Para

con r

ca

The Illustrator

By

Daniela Madrazo

iUniverse, Inc.
New York Bloomington

The Illustrator

iUniverse books may be ordered through booksellers or by contacting:
iUniverse
1663 Liberty Drive
Bloomington, IN 47403
www.iuniverse.com
1-800-Authors (1-800-288-4677)

ISBN: 978-1-4502-3156-5 (pbk)
ISBN: 978-1-4502-3157-2 (ebk)

Printed in the United States of America
iUniverse rev. date: 6/28/10

1

As the old rusty bus stopped with a loud thud in a stop it had never made before, I looked out the window to find out what was going on and why in god's name we had to stop! I waited for a comment like, "Sorry kids, but our good old bus stopped dead! You'll arrive late to school because we have to fix this junk!" but it never came. As I was ripped out of my thinking by the honking of the bus, I saw a girl come out of a yellow house running towards the bus. She was different from all the girls in my school. She was blonde, rather white and pale, and simply different.

As she clumsily climbed on to the bus, she said panting, "I'm so, so sorry! I'm not used to being picked up at this time!".

"Look kid, I know it's the first day of school, but you got to be on time. 'Stood?"

"Yeah! Sorry!" she replied nervously.

Without thinking twice, the girl sat in the first seat she could find as fast as possible. Weird. Very weird. These types of things never happen in Winesburg, Ohio- AKA... here. This is the kind of place were nothing changes and not much happens. So having a new girl in school is like having a rain drop in the middle of a terrible drought.

Thinking so much made me hungry, so I took out my three year old lunch box and opened the zipper calmly. In there, I found a PB & J, a bag of chips and carrot sticks. Posted in my water bottle, was a pink Post-it. Oh no! Guess what it was... A good-luck-on-your-first-day-of-school note. Mom. I grabbed it, made it into a little ball and shoved it quickly into my pocket. I hope no one saw me. They would probably call me something like: "Mommy´s little baby" and that I couldn´t stand. I don´t have the best reputation at school, but I´m not the nerd that gets picked on. I´m ok, and believe me, I want to keep it that way!

***

Math is probably one of the most boring subjects on the planet! I was literally falling asleep! As my eyes closed and I started to lose sense, I was abruptly awaken by Mr. Copmik, "Mr. Chase Russell what is the answer?!" I jumped savagely without knowing what was going on.

"Wha´?" I responded quickly.

"Please don´t snooze in my class Mr. Russell!"

For the rest of the class, I paid complete attention to the boring lesson. When the bell rang, I sighed with relief and stumbled my way out of the classroom.

Finally, it was lunch time, my favorite part of the day. Not only because I get to eat and not be in class, but it´s the small time of the day in which I get to do one of my favorite things…write! I´m writing a book to make money. Not for myself though, but for my family. We are not poor, but it sure would be nice to eat something apart from PB&J every day. So it´s a win-win. I do what I love to do, and my family gets money benefits.

***

As I was doing my homework, I heard muffled voices in my mother´s room. I lay my pencil on my desk, put science homework out of my head, and walked out of my blue room silently. As I gently tip-toed to my mom´s room, I put my ear on the door, slightly brushing it, ready to listen.

"Mary! We can´t afford this! We have enough problems already with the taxes!"

"Ryan calm down! I´ll go down to the diner on Friday´s if you want. Maybe they´ll pay me more and I can ask Donna for an advance!"

I lifted my ear from the white door slowly. Without thinking a lot about what I had just heard, I returned to my room. I slowly sat down in my wooden chair as I thought, *"I have to be quick with my book."*

I slipped into my pajamas and got into bed. I started to fall asleep, as millions of things swarmed crazily in my head.

The next morning, the same girl hopped onto the bus, but this time she wasn't late. She smiled at the driver and said, "Good morning!" which made him blush. As she walked past me she said, "Hi!" in a fairly high pitched voice that did not seem to be hers.

I was sitting on the left side of the bus. The peculiar and yet appealing girl sat on the right side, one seat behind mine. She took a notebook, pencil and iPod out of her bag. She plucked in the earphones, and started scribbling on her paper. I wondered what she was writing, or maybe she was just doodling. Who knows, a girl as weird and bizarre as her could do just about anything.

The movements of her hand and pencil were smooth, curved and balanced. Something in her movements made me relax by neck and body. Instantly, it was as if our thinking connected because her facial traits also started to soften. She once or twice tilted her head from side to side, looking at different perspectives of her work. She caught me looking at her, so I looked away and acted as if I were casually biting my nails. In the corner of my eye, I saw that she looked out the window, blankly, then smiled and returned to her work.

***

I was walking in the hallway, looking at my schedule to see what class I had today, "*7th Grade History.*" I don´t have any problem with this class. It gives me ideas for my stories. Thousands of kids were rushing to their classes, hoping they would get there on time. I saw the number 209 on my schedule. When I looked up, it was right in front of me. On the door was posted a funny cartoon of a prehistoric man. Under that it said, *"Ms.Zelther."* When I read the name, I imagined a fat, old teacher who´s breath would smell like a rotten egg. As I entered the class I was surprised, for there was no fat, old teacher that would make me have a tough year. Instead, I found myself in the class of a beautiful young teacher with curvy black hair and beautiful blue eyes.

"Hi! Are you in my class this year?" she asked. It took me a moment to respond.

"Yeah! I guess?" I answered.

She laughed a little, and then said, "Ok! Then please take a seat!"

As the bell rang, the girl from the bus walked casually into the classroom. Ms. Zelther smiled at her and gestured her to go to her desk.

"Class!" she said."We have a new girl this year! What´s your name, honey?" she asked.

"Um, hi. I´m Bailey Gray."

"All right then, have a seat Bailey," Ms. Zelther responded.

Bailey smiled at the class, and then took a seat. *Bailey Gray,* I thought. *So that´s her name.* For the rest of the class, Ms. Zelther told us about her teaching methods and how the year would work. When the bell rang, I went to my locker to leave my history books and grab my English ones. As I got into my English classroom, it turned out that I had Bailey in this class too.

When Ms. Nacker asked us if anyone had "encountered" with the new girl, she also asked us if anyone knew her name. Without even thinking, the words spilled out of my mouth.

"Her name is Bailey… Bailey Gray."

I was sort of embarrassed for it came out to fast. Bailey seemed to notice, and she said, "Yes. In fact that is my name."

When she was walking to her seat, I gestured a thank you face. All she did was smile, and then she kept walking to her seat.

***

At lunch, I went to the library to write a little more of my book. I sat down with a boy I did not know, since all the other tables were full to the top.

"Hi," I said in a casual voice.

"Hi," the boy said.

He was a red-head, with brown eyes and his nose was sharp.

"Name´s Gordon!" he said.

I thought he might be trying to start a friendly conversation.

"My name is Chase," I responded. "Is it okay if I sit with you?"

"Sure. No problem."

When I looked at Gordon´s shirt I couldn´t help but laugh. It said I MAY LOOK STUPID BUT AT LEAST I´M CIVILIZED!

"What?" he asked quickly.

"Nothing. It's just that your shirt is kind of funny!"

"Oh…Thanks!" he responded.

As I started to talk to Gordon, I discovered that I had just made a new friend.

2

"The adventurer Heath Hanes is trapped! The harahokey have captured him! As they carried him on a stick, Hanes can detect the roasted odor of lava from a volcano! And not just any volcano…the Segdufe volcano! The biggest one in this terrible island Heath had discovered. With his wonderful ability, Heath Hanes reached out for his knife and… JIIIIIIIIIIIICK! I ripped my paper out, for I didn´t like what I had written. I crushed it into a ball and scored it into the trashcan.

"You can´t rip out your work!" Samuel cautioned. Samuel has been my best friend since third grade. He has brown hair, green eyes and he´s a bit zaftig, which means he´s not skinny. He also wears glasses.

"Yeah! Don´t put so much pressure on yourself!" insisted Gordon.

"Ugh! I can´t think! I´m just not able write!"

Both Samuel and Gordon started to laugh. Suddenly, the situation which had seemed so grave before became a little ridiculous. I had to smile, and I too, joined them into the laughing.

"What! I´m serious," I chuckled.

"So what is this book you´re writing about?" Gordon asked.

"You want to know the truth?" I said, "I HAVE NO IDEA!"

"That´s not going to get you anywhere you know," Samuel said.

"Why are you so negative?" I asked.

"I´m not being negative! I´m just facing the facts!" Sam said.

"It´s just that… I haven´t written anything I like! All my writing has been for nothing. I don´t like it, so I rip it and start again! The problem is-" I was stuck, "That I´ve ripped every piece I have done."

"Maybe you should take a break, you know." Gordon said.

"Yeah! Get the book thing out of your head!" replied Samuel.

Maybe I should, I thought. "So! Who´s up for pizza?" I asked.

"I am!" Gordon said.

"Me too!" Samuel added.

So we went down to the kitchen to order. We sat down in the tall chairs, next to the cupboard table. I grabbed the phone, and dialed the *Domino's Pizza* number. "Hi. Um, could I have two large pizzas ...Cheese please...yeah... yeah both of them...Harley Road...number sixteen... Alright! Thank you!" I hung up the phone. "They'll be here in about 25 minutes" I informed.

"Good 'cuz I'm starving!" Samuel said. He said this in a tone that defined his hunger. And when Samuel is hungry, there's no arguing.

"So," I said starting the conversation. "What do you think about the new girl?"

"Weird."

"Odd."

"Different." I said. To Samuel and Gordon this was sort of a spontaneous and unexpected reply. Their answers being *weird* and *odd* and mine being *different* gave them a clue that I found the girl kind of interesting and not totally dorky, eccentric. Their faces expressed bewilderness.

"Wait, what do you mean by different?"Samuel asked.

"I mean we don't know her yet...you know!"It sounded as if I were protecting Bailey from a terrible dragon.

"Dude! Haven't you seen her happy-go-lucky act?! It's like she's in a trance of joy and contentment!" Gordon remarked.

"Yeah but, it kind of makes her stand out," I stumbled on my words.

"Are you saying that you *like* her?" asked Samuel.

"NO!" I said. The volume of my voice was louder than I wanted it to be. "I´m just curious!" I said trying to recover myself. Just as my ship was sinking, the pizza guy saved my life. As the doorbell rang, I collapsed out of my chair, running to the door. The guy on the door step had his Domino´s Pizza smock, two pizzas in his hands and a long, red beard.

"You Chase Russell?" he asked in a low voice.

"That´s me," I said catching my breath.

"Ok. That´ll be twenty dollars- Plus tip," he added.

I stuck my hand into my pocket and flipped out the money. Shoot! I only had two five´s. "Hey guys, could I borrow some money? I really don´t have enough."

"Sure, no problem," they said in unison, and they too took out five´s and cents. We paid the money, tip and all.

"Thank you!" I said as the guy mounted on his motorcycle.

"Anytime," He responded, and rode out into the driveway.

We ate the pizzas very fast, and Samuel chugged up half of one all by himself! We all mumbled things like "*ugh*" and "*I´m so full!*"To digest this much pizza we would take a century. We saw a movie, and then Sam and Gordon went home. After all, it was Sunday, and middle school wasn´t easy.

The fall of feudalism? Did that even happen?!I´m totally going to flunk! I want to make a good impression on Mrs. Zelther…darn is she pretty…Oh! Snap out of it Chase you´re studying here! All of these things hit my head hard as I walked in the hallway studying hard for my ancient history test. I wasn´t even watching were I was going. My eyes were focused blindly on my paper.

I wasn´t paying much attention at the people walking around me... or in front of me. In an instant, I crashed into Bailey! She was carrying a number of books, papers, pencils and pens all which ended scattered on the floor. For a moment it was like blacking out. When I finally came to my senses I looked around to find both of us on the floor. The mystery was discovered. Her scribbling on the bus came down to this. In plain pencil, there were wonderful drawings of various things. Quickly skimming, I saw a goose, a flower, a bus stop, a dog and a house that looked just like Bailey´s.

I gathered the pages together and gave them to Bailey, "You dropped these," I said and my voice quivered. I hated the way it all came out.

"Yeah, I think I noticed that. Are you ready for the test?"

"Do I look ready?" I asked.

"No, not exactly," Bailey said.

"I´ll walk you to class," I said, "Those are amazing drawings!" I wasn´t lying. They were very good.

"Thanks," she answered.

After the bell rang I got the most relieving news. The test had been postponed to Wednesday because the printer broke. Phew!

***

At dinner, dad´s face looked shady and tired. His hair was ruffled, and his eyes had circles underneath them behind his glasses. Mom just had a worried look on her face. "Is something wrong?" I asked between a mouthful of peas.

"Well, for us money and problems are synonyms," Dad said as he nabbed his face and eyes in utter exhaustion.

"Are the taxes higher?" asked Ben, my older brother. He´s sixteen, and a complete teenager.

"What´s a tax?"Michael asked. Ben rolled his eyes and returned to his food. Michael is my younger brother. He´s five, and completely unaware that our money is tight.

"It´s an amount of money that you pay for the services you get. It benefits the government or other people," my mother explained. Her voice quivered too. And it sounded just like me. There was dead silence at the table except for the sound of food being chewed. Mom and dad exchanged a look that I knew would lead to some conversation…and it did.

"Guys, we have something to tell you. The money we have is somewhat fair, but sometimes it doesn´t make the cut. We can´t buy a new car or anything like that," my dad explained, "From now on, you guys will be doing some chores around here. That´ll give your mother and me a chance to work a little more and get money." Mom grabbed dad´s had and stroked it with her thumb. I started to feel uncomfortable with the theme that was picked for tonight. *Don't go any further* I thought. Dad read my mind and stopped. There was an uncomfortable silence. "You can all start by washing your dishes," Dad ended. Mom hadn´t said a word. Both my parents went upstairs.

"It´s obvious isn´t it?" Ben said.

"What is?" I asked. Stupid question. I knew that.

"What else, Chase? We´re obviously in a money wreck!" Ben turned off the water and put his piece of old china in the drying rack. "If you´ll excuse me!" he said obnoxiously. Ben trampled out of the kitchen with a skeptical look on his face.

"Chase, I can´t reach the sink. Could you help me?" Michael asked.

"Sure. I´ll wash your plate for you. How does that sound?" I answered.

"Thanks Chase! I owe you one," Michael said and skipped out of the kitchen. My brothers were so different from each other.

When I finished washing Mike´s dish, I turn of the water, dried my hands with an old rag and sighed. In my room I lay in bed, thinking to myself: *What a dinner I just had.*

The next morning, Bailey got on the bus and sat next to me without even asking. She just smiled the smile she used frequently, and looked away. It was a line of bright white teeth that sparkled with the sun. It was that type of smile that lifted you spirits up. We did not talk at all. Bailey did her identical morning routine. Plug in earphones, open notebook, get out pencil, and draw. This time, she drew my hand resting on my lap. It was so good; it could have been a photograph.

When she finished, she put away her notebook and said, "Chase right?"

"Yeah," I answered.

"I´m Bailey."

"I know," I responded, regretting it instantly.

"Hmmm-" she said.

"What?" I asked.

"Could you look out the window, and just stay there for a moment," she said while she took out her notebook out again.

"Okay," I said awkwardly and I looked out the window. All I heard was scribble, scribble, erase, scribble, scribble. At the end of the bus ride, she said thank you and got off the bus.

As I was walking in to the Winesburg Middle School building, I saw Jeremy Hirsch with his friends, talking and laughing. Jeremy Hirsch is the eighth grade bully, quite a vagarious student, and I hate him. As I passed by him, one of his friends grabbed my backpack and pulled me into the crowd.

"Hey short stack! What are you doin′ here?" Jeremy said.

"Aren′t you like in second grade?" asked one of his friends named Paul Avery. They all laughed.

"We′ll for your four one one, Hirsch I′m in seventh grade," I said.

"Oh! He′s so smart!" Jeremy said in baby talk.

"Yeah, I do think I′m smart and that′s because I have a brain. And your brain must be the size of a poppy seed!" I shouted. Jeremy smirked.

"You think you're all grown, don't cha? Think you′re quick, too?" he said.

"Maybe I do, Jeremy Hirsch. Got a problem with that?!" I asked defensively. My voice in this scene sounded brave and strong, but inside I was shaking like a Chihuahua. This guy was dangerous, and I am terrible at defending myself.

"Yeah I do! You piss me off! Here, consider it a free welcome present." Jeremy Hirsch took out of his mouth a piece of pink, chewed gum, and stuck it in my hair. Hirsch, Avery and company walked away, laughing hysterically. I heard them say things like "*Good one, Jeremy,*" and "*We′ll get that kid later!*"

Bailey crept up on me and said, "Sorry about that. Want help?" she asked.

"I′m fine thanks!" I said harshly and rapidly.

"Well, catch you later," She said sheepishly and walked away.

I went inside the boy's bathroom to get the piece of gum out of my hair. A boy that appeared to be in eighth grade came out of one of the bathrooms. "Hirsch and Avery?" He asked looking at my hair.

"Yep," I answered.

The eighth grader sighed, pushed the bathroom door and walked out. I turned on the water and wet my hands. I pulled out carefully the piece of gum from the strand of hair it was stuck on and threw it to the trash.

At the end of class, Ms. Zelther told me to go to her desk. I shuffled forward and remained silent.

"I heard you had a little bully encounter this morning," she said. I hesitated. "Look Chase; don't let those kids put you down. You know better than that," Ms. Zelther said. I just nodded. "Come on. Get going or you'll be late for your next class!"

I walked to the door slowly. "Ms. Zelther," I said. She turned around. "Thanks." I said, and I walked out the door.

***

In the afternoon, Bailey did the same thing she had done in the morning. She sat next to me without asking. "Were did you live before you came here?" I asked when she sat down.

"Um, hi. I'm fine thank you," she said.

"Sorry. HI! Are you good now?" I asked.

"Yes, thank you. Now, you may talk."

"Okay! Where did you live?" I asked for the second time.

"Well, I came from California," She said.

"What´s it like?" I wondered.

"Like… this," she said and she took out a drawing of a beautiful house on the coast of a beach. There was another picture on the back, but this time, it was a picture of a room´s balcony.

"This is really cool! But what is this balcony?" I asked.

"That´s the front view of my old room. You opened those like, windows, and you went out to this like, porch slash balcony. It was really cool."

For the first time I noticed the man that was drawn smiling on the balcony.

"Who´s that?" I asked curiously.

"That´s my dad. I got him to pose for the drawing," she said.

The closer I looked at the picture, the more curious I grew about Bailey´s life.

"Will I get to meet your dad some day?" I asked.

"We´ll see," she replied without any trace of commitment.

3

In the past few days, I concluded some things about Bailey: Either she was stalking me, or I have personal space issues in which she gave me ideas without even noticing. The drawing of that beautiful place inspired me and I officially knew what my book would be about. It would be about a boy that accidentally discovers this magical place and makes fantastic, fictional friends.

I called Gordon and Samuel to give them the good news. They also liked the idea. Gordon gave me a not so good opinion. He was obviously distracted when he gave it to me. Samuel gave me the academic and professional opinion. Sam is all academics. Gordon is all himself.

Since Bailey adopted the idea of sitting next to me, I didn´t fight it and just let her do it. I didn´t mind. Before, our bus rides consisted on a slight and friendly *hello,* followed by silence. Now, we actually talked. We didn´t converse deeply, but at least we did have a slight communication.

Her weird habits did not wear off, though. She still smiled at people that were mean to her, she still shot up her hand violently when she knew an answer and she still appeared spontaneously where ever I was.

I was not annoyed by it anymore. I even sought to it. I liked to guess where I would find her next or when she would appear at my side.

"Hey!" I said the next morning when Bailey sat in her seat.

"Hi." She replied sheepishly and shortly. She pulled a package of Starburst candies out of her bag. "Want one?" she asked unwrapping the one, little square she had taken herself.

"Thanks," I said taking a pink one.

"This is my favorite candy in the entire world!" Bailey announced.

"Really?" I asked.

"Yeah, what yours?" she wondered.

"Hmm- Probably Skittles," I answered.

"Hey! I´ve got an idea! How about we name all our favorite things?" Bailey said.

"Okay. Let's start with favorite color," I said.

"My favorite color is blue. All types of blue," she said.

"Mine´s green," I compared.

"Okay, now, favorite animal," Bailey suggested.

"Mine's a giraffe."

"Mine's a goose!"

"So that explains the sketch of that goose you made," I said.

"You are correct! Now, favorite chocolate bar!" Bailey put down, "Milky Way."

"Snickers," I affirmed. We went on and on. For favorite food, I picked pizza as Bailey selected Jell-O! Favorite type of book, we both picked fiction. What a coincidence. Favorite subject: I picked English/ Language Arts. Bailey picked Art class. That didn't really count as a subject, but her pick was obvious. Favorite song, music, band, movie, and favorite place in the world, we couldn't decide. It was a fun conversation I had with Bailey. We laughed a lot, while joking around our options.

During science, Bailey passed me a little paper. It was a funny cartoon of Ms. Stein the oh so boring teacher. I put the drawing inside my folder in the science tab. I'm very organized with my things, and I have a tab folder. My folder has one section for each subject, and each section has a tab with the name of the subject. In my room everything is neat and tidy. The clothes in my closet all faced the same way, and my desk is perfectly clean. I'm a little too neat for a middle school boy. Samuel is ordered but not as much as me. And Gordon, well, he's a mess.

As the teacher went on and on talking about ribonucleic acid (what the heck is that?!), I wrote the beginning of my story. I decided that the boy´s name would be Peter, and the place with a magical world would be called Swordenslane Island. There would be fairies, trolls, elves, unicorns, dragons, and gnomes! Here is what I wrote in science:

"Peter! Come on, we already ~~finidhe~~ finished packing up the truck!" Peter was an 8 year old boy with dark, black hair and deep blue eyes. He loved his Connecticut house more than anything. But now he was moving to a house in the coast of California, next to the beach. His dad had gotten a job there. Peter felt sorrow in his soul. He did not want to go, and he had done many things to stop himself from leaving. He tied himself to a tree outside with a rope, he glue-gunned himself to a chair, and many other crazy things. But ~~now~~ this time, all he did was walk down the stairs with his suitcase.

I liked it. The bell rang. Thank god! When we walked out the door, Bailey asked, "What were you doing?" It was about time Bailey knew.

"I am writing a novel, a book in other words," I said proud of myself. "And I have to thank you because that drawing you showed me of your old house in California, well, it inspired me and now I know what I´ll write about. So, thank you." I finished.

"Well then, you´re welcome!" she said and she skipped off.

I wondered if later on she would give me other ideas with her imagination and pieces of art.

***

The days passed, and it was Saturday. Mom, the order freak (I probably got it from her), had made a chart of the new chores we were supposed to do. Michael, of course, had the easiest chores with the excuse that he is five, and a disaster. On the other hand, Ben and I have all the boring and tough chores.

I went to the name column all the way down to my name. Then I moved my finger right to the Saturday column. I had to turn on the sprinklers on the front yard, collect the dirty laundry baskets and take them to the washing machine, and last but not least, wash the car. I decided to start them that very moment, that way I could get them over with.

I put on a grey hoodie over my pajamas and headed outside. I pushed the sprinklers into the grass and turned them on. On my way back into the house, I got soaking wet. Then one by one I gathered up the laundry baskets. I separated them the way I was supposed to. Whites, blacks and dark colors, prints, and normal colors. I dumped the basket of whites into the washing machine first. Then, I put in one cup of Tide detergent, and started the washer. Next, I went outside, *again,* turned off the sprinklers and washed the car. I turned on the hose and washed off the pick-up's dirt nonchalantly. Since we did not have any fancy soap for the car, I just scrubbed it with a sponge. *Ugh* I thought.

After I finished with my tedious chores, it was writing time! I ran up the stairs making loud thuds with each step I took. I tripped and fell at the fifth step. I am a bit clumsy some times, but not constantly. That is one of the reasons why I´m so neat. All I did was laugh at myself and stand up. I finished climbing the last couple of stairs, and jogged to my room. I closed the door quickly and headed for my desk. I pulled the drawer where I usually put my writing notebook. What? Where was it? I considered my options. A) Michael thought it was a drawing utensil. B) I "misplaced it." C) I left it at school. D) Ben was finding another way to mock me more than he already did.

First, Michael wouldn´t dare to even touch my things. Not A. Not B, because I´m simply a neat freak. Not C, because of the same reason as B. So only one option was left…D. I stampeded to the room next to mine. I didn´t bother knocking on the door. I flung it open with all my strength. As the door bounced on the wall, I saw Ben sitting on the edge of his bed with my notebook in his hands, a wicked smile spread across his face.

"Well, well, well, Chase. What is this?!" He asked amused. He grabbed my notebook in his left hand and shook it as if he were in a Broadway show.

"What´s the matter with you? Do you think I´m going to play doggie catch or something? Give- it- back!" my voice was hard.

"Come and get it!" Ben sung.

My face turned crimson red with anger and my jaw clenched tightly. "Give it back!" I shouted again between gritted teeth.

“This is so ridiculous!”Ben snickered. “Peter felt sorrow in his soul?” he quoted. “What the heck is THAT?!” Ben started laughing so hard he was hitting the bed with his fist, like an old cartoon.

I couldn´t help it. I sprinted toward him and punched his nose indefinitely hard. I stood there shocked for a moment, ripped my notebook out of Ben´s hands as he reached for his nose in pain. I ran out my stupid brother´s room. I threw the notebook inside my own room harshly and rushed down the stairs.

I opened the main door and slammed it shut. I needed a walk. Whenever my patience runs out or I have an emotional breakdown, nothing can calm me down more than a walk with me, myself, and I. My arms were folded next to my chest in agony. The sound of my feet hitting the pavement on the sidewalk was the only one I could listen to. I sat on a bench that was in front of a house that looked almost the same as my own. I took a deep breath and then let out a long sigh. I tried to close my eyes but if I did, the scene I had just been through replayed in my mind. So I chose to keep walking.

As I scrambled for reasons to my actions, I saw white, fury dot running towards me. As it got nearer, I noticed that it was a dog running crazily with its tongue hanging out for breath. It was the type of ruffled dog that if you glued a stick on its back, it could be a mop. The dog stopped right in front of me, scrambling and zigzagging through my legs.

I had seen this dog before but…where? As I thought, almost in a blink, Bailey appeared around the corner running with a leash in her hand.

"Luna!" she called.

The dog didn´t mind responding. It just hid behind me. I patted its side in amusement. Bailey came to a stop in front of me. She was panting heavily.

"Luna! Why on earth did you do that?!" she snapped quickly. The dog whimpered behind me.

"Hey, Bails. Is this dog yours?" I asked.

"Hi, Chase. Yeah. That´s Luna," she answered.

When I took the dog in my arms, it looked as if Luna grinned at me. "I like her name. How did you come up with it?" I asked.

"Well, in Spanish, *Luna* means moon," She explained.

"Oh. It´s pretty cool!" I said.

"Thanks," She replied.

It finally came to me. This dog was one of the drawings that Bailey had the day I slammed into her. "Is that the dog you drew?" I asked.

"Yeah!" she answered.

"So then I´ve discovered most of your drawing mysteries. The dog is Luna; the goose is your favorite animal, the bus stop, well- it´s your bus stop, and then your house is the drawing of the house," I said, "But there is still one drawing I haven't quite discovered yet: the flower," I finished.

"Oh, that!" she said. Pause. She reflected by looking at something that was at a distance. She did not move her absent gaze but she answered, "That was just doodling, really… yeah, pretty much!" she answered, and then returned her gaze back at me.

She smiled. I hadn't noticed how beautifully her face was structured. Her deep, blue, swirling eyes were like sapphires that burned my eyes. I shut my own to reduce the burning feeling.

"What's wrong?" she asked in a worried tone. Her face was preoccupied.

"Nothing. I'm fine," I said.

"So, why are you out here?" she questioned, grabbing Luna from my arms, taking her into her own.

"Well, my brother, Ben, took my writing notebook to bother me, I got really angry, and I punched him across the face, and decided to take a walk." Bailey's face was perplexed. I continued, "Walking calms me down, like a sleeping pill. I can think things over," I sighed.

"Oh. I was just giving Luna here a walk and she broke out of her leash," Bailey explained. "Do you want to keep walking with me?" she asked.

When people ask you those types of questions, you answer yes or no and that's it. Period. But inexplicably, I felt butterflies batting at my stomach to the question. Why was nervous? "Sure!" my voice quivered, giving me away. *Shoot!* I thought.

We walked down to the pond in the neighborhood and sat by my favorite cider tree. I was big and old. When at it, it looked wise.

"Wow! Cool tree," She said.

"Yeah, I love it. I´ve come to this tree since I was like, five," I said.

"It´s amazing." she pointed out.

"Did you finish Ms. Zelther´s homework?" I asked.

"Yeah, and Ms. Nacker's stupid 'use of punctuation' essay," as she said this, she motioned quotation marks around the words *use of punctuation.*

I laughed. "What was your life in California like?" I asked her.

"Well, scorching heat, beaches, and my house was on the coast-" she stopped. "I had a lot of friends there, but it was hard to get them," she replied, "since people think I´m, really weird…I had to show them the real me. The real Bailey," she finished.

"So it must be hard for you to start all over again," I answered.

Her expression started to look a little bit sad. "Yeah. New house, new school, new people, and new place-" she continued, "Thanks," she said.

"For what?" I questioned.

"For being my friend. You made my start easier."

We kept talking, occasionally laughing at something one of us remarked. The day went by in a blur, and none of us noticed that the night had caught up with us.

"Shoot!" Bailey exclaimed. "It´s 7:00pm and neither of us went home for dinner!" She gasped and put a hand to her face.

I noticed what had happened. "My parents must be worrying sick!" I said.

"Oh my gosh! Let´s go!" Bailey exclaimed.

We both scrambled to our feet.

"See you, Chase!" she said running in the direction of her house.

"Yeah! See you, Bails!" I said.

I rushed down to the door on my own house and quickly got inside. My whole family was sitting at the table, already done with dinner.

"Where on earth have you been, Chase Russell?" my father questioned.

"Sorry, Dad. I was with a friend," I told him. Of course, I didn´t mind telling them what friend it was.

"You must be starving! You didn´t come for dinner!" she said preoccupied. She is SO motherly.

"I´m fine, mom," I said.

"I don´t care if he´s starving or not! He isn´t going to get dinner and that´s the end of this conversation! Now, go up to your room! You won´t get out of there unless I let you!" my father finished.

I didn´t bother arguing. I nodded once, hovered a bit, and walked upstairs. I absentmindedly put on my pajamas and got into bed. There I lay, looking at the ceiling, my arms pinned to my side.

Suddenly, the door opened a fraction and Michael came in with a plate in his hands.

"Mike?" I asked.

"Hey, Chase! I brought you some food!" he whispered, closed the door behind him silently, and walked to my side.

"Here, I have to go now."

It turned out my saving meal was a messily made cheese sandwich.

"Thanks Mike!"

He smiled, and left the room. I ate quickly and hid the plate under my bed. At least I had a nice brother.

4

“PB and J, saltines, and an apple,” I informed as Gordon, Sam, Jack, and I listed the content of our lunchboxes. Jack, a tall boy with black hair and amber eyes had joined our crew. He sat with us in lunch and talked to me in math class. Personally, I liked Jack. He was a great listener… as well as a big talker. He did not stop!

My school is pretty much like any typical school you see in movies. In the cafeteria, our present location, there were round and rectangular grey, plastic tables. In the isolated and round table in the corner of the cafeteria sat Bailey, alone as usual. *Should invite her to eat with us?* I made my decision.

When she looked up, I waved at her and gestured her to come. She nodded once and tried to hide a smile. She packed her lunch up and glided towards us.

“What are you doing?!”Gordon asked.

“She is really nice. Trust me,” I said.

"Hey, guys!" Bailey saluted.

"Hey, Bails!"

My friend´s faces were structured in disbelief.

"May I join you?" she asked.

"Sure," Jack answered, helping me out.

Samuel snarled. I narrowed my eyes and shot a look at him. He got my point.

"Welcome, Bailey!" he said nervously and shaky.

"God, you are stupid," I said under my breath. He raised an eyebrow and slightly bit his lip.

"Anyway," Jack interfered.

"Sit down, sit down," Gordon said.

She smiled showing a row of great, white teeth.

"Thanks!" she said.

Bailey grabbed a shinny, red apple and took a bite.

Um, well I was thinking that maybe you could, uh, tell us something about you," Samuel said.

"She´s an amazing drawer, you know," I said.

They were all staring at me between mouthfuls of lunch. They could not believe my attempts to making Bailey "feel at home."

"Er, cool! Let´s see it then!" Jack said.

Bailey wasn´t buying it.

"Um, sure," she said and she took out of her pocket the drawing of her California house.

She put it in the middle of the table and patted it. Jack, Sam, and Gordon leaned in to take a closer look. Their eyes widened and they all said in unison, "Wow!" mouthing every letter in a dumbstruck tone.

"I´m kind of getting hungry. I think I´ll go get a pizza slice or something," Bailey said.

She grabbed her tray of food and walked to the food bar.

"You guys are SO lame!" I said pausing briefly in between words; a hint of sarcasm in it.

I started laughing. They all scowled at me, and I scowled back. Samuel and Jack where facing the food bar and Gordon sat with his back towards it, like me.

"She´s peeking," Sam said through unmoving lips.

"She wasn´t really believing it you know," I said.

"Houston, we have a problem! She´s coming back!" Samuel warned through his teeth.

"Change the subject!" Jack whispered urgently.

"Do you like flowers?" Gordon said out loud, attempting to accomplish Jack´s request.

I snorted and slapped a hand on my forehead. We all managed to suppress our snickers as Bailey sat down.

"I thought you were getting pizza," I said.

"Oh. I just really- I can´t eat pizza," she said.

"Why not? Too many calories?" Gordon said mocking her.

"No. I´m…I´m lactose intolerant," she spat.

"Oh, wow. It must be tough for you," Samuel said.

"You have no idea!" Bailey assured us all.

As lunch flew by, Bailey won my guys over, just like she had with me. She had a natural glimmer and charm. She could soften anything and anyone with her sweet eyes and caring self. When the bell rang, my friends were still in deep conversation with her. That was until Bailey broke it up by saying, "Well, see you guys later!" and she strode off.

"Just took her one lunch period to snap your traps, huh?" I said.

"Well, she´s- nice," Sam said.

So now the problem of my friends not liking Bailey was resolved… Thank God! Now everyday she sat with us, chatting and talking. We were all growing fond of Bailey, especially me.

One day, Bailey came to our table but she wasn´t alone. She came with a brunette girl, with wavy hair who was also pretty. They were talking and laughing.

"Hey, guys! This is Natalie!" Bailey said when she reached the table.

"Hi," Natalie said."Can I sit with you?"

"Sure!" Gordon answered.

Jack´s jaw was open in awe.

"Jack, earth is calling," I said waving a hand across his face.

He shook his head to wake up. Natalie giggled and sat down. Natalie was really nice. And Bailey had picked a good friend. Jack was obviously struck by the fact of Amanda being attractive. When Bails and Amanda left for Geo, Jack managed to drop his jaw even lower.

"Natalie-is-perfect!" he exclaimed.

"Oh, get a grip of yourself!"Gordon said.

We laughed. We cut into two groups. Me and Jack off to Math with Copmik, while Gordon and Sam headed for Gym. We all kind of suck at sports, except for Jack; he's athletic man, and I'm kind of jealous of him. He's athletic, tall, very handsome, smart, well, he's pretty much good at everything. Me, not really- I'm trash at everything. Except for writing, and being quiet, and ordered. My mom says I have social skills but those don't really count.

So then it was Math, as usual, same boring thing. How can people NOT get these things? They're so easy! Jack wasn't paying attention since he was too busy daydreaming about Natalie. Why is this class so boring?

The rest of the day was thoroughly long, like it would never end. In a period of time it did, and I went home.

When I got on the bus to ride, I looked at our seat; Bailey wasn't there. I sat alone waiting for her to come, but she never did. I had the slightest hope of her coming until the bus driver closed the door, and started the engine. On the way I thought of reasons for Bailey's absence. It was useless to try, in the end, because I ran out of ideas.

When I got home, I called the number Bailey had given me days ago. There were three rings, and then a sweet and smooth voice answered, *"Hello! Gray residence!"*

"Hi, um, is Bailey home?"I asked.

"Who's this?" the voice asked.

"I'm Chase," I said.

"Oh! Hello, Chase! Yeah, she's right here."

I waited for a moment and then Bailey's voice appeared, huskier than usual. *"Hey, Chase,"* she croaked.

"Hi, Bails. Why weren't you on the bus today at the end of school?" I asked.

"Well, in lunch Natalie gave me some type of biscuit to try it. I didn't know it had milk in it and I just started...feeling bad," she finished.

"What happens to you if you drink milk?" I asked.

She sighed and said, *"It's kind of embarrassing...I- when you're lactose intolerant and you drink milk, your stomach literally-blows up! You get all bottled up with gas and-you fart."*

I held back a laugh by covering my mouth. There was a silent pause.

"What, you're not going to laugh?" she asked amused.

"Actually, I did but I covered my mouth for your own sake," I said.

She laughed. *"Well, thanks for calling, Chase,"* she said.

"No problem. I was forced into it!" I joked.

"Oh, I know you weren't! Bye," she said, and she hung up.

I held my breath as I hung up as well. I snorted at our conversation and smiled. I climbed the stairs by two's and entered my room. I flipped over the sign on my door to the side that said *DO NOT DISTURB!* , and closed the door. Only seconds later when I had barely managed to sit down in my chair, the door opened and Ben was in the doorway.

"I thought I flipped the sign to the side that says 'DO NOT DISTURB!' Didn't you read it?" I asked quite annoyed.

"Actually I did but I assumed that since I'm your brother you would be willing to remove some boundaries for me," he answered.

"What do you want, Ben?" I asked.

"Oh, nothing. Just came to mingle with my favorite little brother!" he kept taunting.

"Well, I'm kind of busy so you won't get lots of *mingling* from me," I snapped.

"Oh, what are you busy with?" he interrogated.

"Have I broken a law or something? I'm just doing homework and stuff," I said.

"That's fine! I'll just sit here and watch you," he said as he flopped onto my bed.

"I'm really not that interesting, you know," I said.

"Never said you were, Chase. I've just got nothing better to do!" he finished.

"Fine. You know what, I'll just ignore you. How does that sound?" I asked.

"Fine by me, Chase, fine by me," my brother said.

At the beginning, Ben didn't talk, and I thought he'd give me the silence therapy to prove me wrong about ignoring him. After what seemed like five minutes, Ben said, "I really can't take this anymore. Silence frustrates me."

He waited for me to say something but I just sat there looking at my math notebook.

"So, do you like any of the girls at school?" he asked.

Shoot! He had caught me off guard! "Do-do you?" I asked.

"Yeah, but I swear, Chase! You tell anyone and I'll kill you and make it look like an accident!" he threatened.

"I cross my heart and hope to die!" I pledged.

"Okay, I like Lindsey Fieldston," he spat out.

That girl in tenth grade was popular, beautiful, and Ben didn't stand a chance.

"She's-pretty," I said.

"She probably doesn't even know I exist!" Ben said.

No, she probably doesn't, I thought, but I wasn't going to say that to my brother. "Oh, don't worry, man! She's probably TOTALLY into you!" I lied.

"Do you really think so?" his face was scrutinized. It was burning me, and I had played all my cards. The only option was to tell him the truth.

"Not…really. But you never know! What if she REALLY likes you but acts like she doesn't?" I encouraged.

"Probably not. It's because Lindsey is so…"

I listened to him intently the first few sentences, but in the middle, my head was already somewhere else. I turned to my math homework and Ben told me, "Are you listening to me?"

"Yeah! I mean, I'm not looking at you but I'm definitely hearing every word you say!"

He kept talking and pouring out his feeling for Lindsey Fieldston. I managed to finish my work.

"Do you think writing a poem and sticking it into her locker is too corny?"

I zapped back to "our" conversation. "A-a little," I said. "It kind of sounds like first grade all over again. You're all shy and shaky about it," I admitted.

"She intimidates me, a little. I feel like she's too good for me and that I'm not good enough!"

This was a Ben that I didn´t know. "You should talk to her. You´re a strong, independent guy and she deserves someone like you," I finished.

"Okay, later, Chase. And, thanks. I really needed to talk to someone."

"Anytime," I said and he walked out of the room.

The phone rang and I picked it up. "*Hello?"* A familiar voice said.

"Bailey?" I asked.

"Hey, Chase! Want to head down to the park?" she asked.

"Aren´t you still blown up like a balloon?" I teased.

"No! I have taken my medicine and I´m okay now."

"Oh, okay. I´ll see you after dinner, okay?" I said. I was a little too pleased by this phone call.

"All right, bye!"

"Bye, Bails," I said.

The moment I hung up, my mother´s voice came from the kitchen."Guys! Food´s ready!"

I walked downstairs and sat at the table. My mother did her daily questionnaire.

"How was school?" she asked,"Fine," we all said in unison.

"Have you all finished your homework?"

That question was for Ben and me, because Michael didn´t have homework yet.

"No," Ben admitted.

"Yes!" I affirmed.

We all chewed up the meal in a quick period of time. As we washed dishes and cleaned up, my mom said her final words.

"Ben, homework. Michael- I don´t know."

"Yay!" Mike said, and ran upstairs waving his hands above his head. Ben resentfully followed to go to his room.

"And, Chase, got any plans for this afternoon?" my mother asked.

"Yes, actually. I was heading down to the-" I cleared my throat, "Park," I finished.

"Oh, you don´t go down there very often," my mom said.

"Well, doesn´t hurt to visit once in a while," I said.

"All right, but be back soon or your father will go nuts!" she warned.

"Okay, bye mom!"I said and walked out the door.

A smile spread across my face as I walked in the direction of the neighborhood park. My walking picked up and turned into jogging. The closer I got, the more I lowered my pace until it became walking again.

Bailey was on a swing, waiting for me. She turned around and said, "Hey, Chase!"

She patted the rusty, old chain of the swing beside her and I sat on it.

"You´re late," she said."Really? I actually thought I would be here before you," I teased.

"I´m kidding," she said.

"So what´s up?" I asked.

"Nothing specifically crucial," She said and we chuckled.

"How long have we been at school?" I questioned.

"That´s...three months and seven days," she calculated.

"You´re pretty up to date," I mocked, "I feel like they flew by."

"Me too," she replied. "So what does that have anything to do with your curiosity of why you are here?" she said.

"Well, I was wondering for how long we have known each other," I admitted.

"Why did you want to know that?" she said.

"Just wondering," I answered.

"Fine then," she said in a sweet tone.

Suddenly, what I had thought about for many days now and longed to ask Bailey came to my head.

"Bails-"

"Yes?"

"Would- would you please be my illustrator?" I looked up to her.

"What do you mean?" she said.

"I mean would you please illustrate my book?"

I waited for her to answer. Her beautiful smile spread across her even more beautiful face.

"Yes!" she said.

She hopped out of her swing and I stud up. She took a step forward and gave me a friendly hug, and I hugged her back. She released me and said, "One thing though, why me?" she asked.

I stared at her in disbelief. "Why not you? You draw spectacularly well and you´re the only reason I even have a story! I was stuck before! The moment I saw the drawing of your old house in California I knew wanted to write!" I explained.

"Well I´m honored!" she responded.

We talked about the book, and how Peter should look like as well as the fairies. We also discussed the other fictional creatures. We parted at 6:30. She gave me a one armed hug and kissed my cheek. I started to blush.

"Thank you. For choosing me. Bye!" she said and she ran back to her house.I stood there, paralyzed. She was glad with my pick, and so was I.

"Bye, Bailey," I muttered silently.

I walked home with my hands in my pockets. When I entered the front door, my mom was making dinner.

"Hi, sweetheart. Had fun all alone at the park?" she said.

"I don´t mind being alone. But I had a great time. Good memories in that place!" I said.

"Good, good," my mother said.

I thought of how there really were great memories at the park, but now, there would be even better ones.

5

In the morning, Bailey already had some sketches of how Peter would look like. They were all great, but I specifically liked one of them. As we entered the building, I got a glimpse of Jeremy Hirsch. He stopped talking with his friends and pointed at Bailey. He said something to them, and then a smile curled on the left corner of his mouth. They all began to laugh and grin.

I took Bailey´s hand and towed her to the stairs, "Come on," I said.

She looked over her shoulder to see the cause of my behavior, but Hirsch and his gang were gone. We had science with Mrs. Stein and we reviewed the types of energy that exist. After that, I had no classes with Bailey.

When I went to my locker to get my books, there was a little note stuck inside the door´s little rims. I pulled it out as I opened my locker. It said: **New people for you to meet today!-Bailey.**

At lunch Bailey appeared not only with Natalie, but with two more girls. They walked together in an equal strut. Their names were MaryAnn and Isabella. MaryAnn had short, sleek, black hair. Isabella had a bronze almost blonde hair that was somewhat wavy like Natalie, whose hair pulled up into a ponytail. We obviously hadn´t noticed them in previous years.

They all turned out well. Samuel´s eyes were on MaryAnn, Gordon´s on Isabella, and Jack´s on Natalie (as usual), and mine were on Bailey. She too had her hair pulled up into a beautifully long, wavy ponytail. One small strand of hair was framing the right side of her face. She looked good in anything!

At the end of lunch period, we all went our separate ways, again. In Gym, I got hit by the ball twice, and I couldn´t kick it. When people shot balls at the goal, or in other words, me, I couldn´t stop a single one. I just put my hands in front of me, and hoped for the best. I ended up running laps for the rest of the class. As I drank water from my bottle, Jack walked up to me.

"Nice running class!" he said.

"Yeah, fun stuff!" I panted.

"Well, maybe next class they´ll just make you walk for your own sake!"

"Shut up!" I said.

A boy named Charlie walked by. "Hey Chase! Had fun running today?" he teased.

"You have no idea!" I said sarcastically.

"Hey could I eat with you guys?" he asked randomly.

"Um, su- sure!" I said with an astonished look. I barely knew this guy!

"Oh, thanks man!" he said, and he walked away.

The next day, in second period I went to English; most commonly known as Mrs. Nacker. The sound of her squeaky shoes and heavy panting approached.

"Woo! Climbing up those stairs sure is a lot of exercise!" Mrs. Nacker.

The woman was probably the oldest citizen in the entire state of Ohio; and one thing is for sure, she´s the size of a hippopotamus!

"Class, we will start our new assignment today," she said.

Everyone groaned

"I know, sounds exciting. You will each write a small novel, more like a short story," she said flatly.

Obviously, she wasn´t very excited either.

"It must five pages long, front and back, and it will be about a fictional creature that you will create which will be composed of two different animals," she explained.

The little light bulb in my head turned on. I would mix a- a cow, with…a blowfish! Yes! It would be called *The Blowcow!* The moment Mrs. Nacker gave out the papers I started writing. My hand and brain were functioning like partners. My hand flowed lickety- split through the paper like wind. In a few minutes I was already getting my next paper, and the next one after that, so on and so forth. At the end of forty five minutes, I put my papers together, stapled them, and turned them in. Mrs. Nacker was correcting some tests at her desk.

"I′m done Mrs. Nacker," I said, and the whole class turned to look at me in disbelief.

Everyone except Bailey. She made a half smile and returned to her work. Ms. Nacker scribbled in a comment and looked at me over her spectacles.

"I hope you didn′t write your abc′s on this paper, Mr. Russell. This has to be good," she warned.

"It is," I answered confidently.

She took the papers and I returned to my seat. The second one to finish was Bailey, as I imagined she would be. There were kids rocking back and forth on their chairs or chewing off the end of their pencils. Everyone was obviously flustered about what to write.

For the rest of the period, people remained working on their stories. It was another eternal period. Mrs. Nacker was able to read my papers, and check them.

When the bell rang, Mrs. Nacker said, "Chase Russell, come here."

I put the strap of my backpack over my shoulder, and walked over to her desk.

"Mr. Russell what is this?" she asked my papers in her hands.

"My- work?" I said.

"When I say what is this I mean this isn´t good," she said.

My eyebrows pulled together in misunderstanding.

"And what I mean by this isn´t good is it's spectacular."

My forehead relaxed and I smiled, "Really?" I asked.

"Yes! It´s brilliant!" she said, "The only thing is that there are some spelling mistakes and I need you to break down some more paragraphs and it´s star quality!"

"Thank you," I said amazed by her reaction.

"You know what, I´ll present it next class as anonymous so you won´t be embarrassed, okay?" she was excited.

"Okay," I said weakly.

"All right, well, run along now," she finished.

I walked out of the classroom happily.

"What did she hold you back for?" Bailey asked.

"She, uh- complimented me on my story," I said.

I accompanied Biley as she slid through the food bar and picked up a bagel. We had to pay for cafeteria food, so I had lunch of my own. We could save up the money and use it at home, or at least that´s what my parents said.

"And?" Bailey said, putting a banana on her tray.

"And she´s going to present it in class- anonymously though," I finished.

"Cool!" she said and we walked back to the table.

Charlie was already sitting there, and he was okay, but he could get really annoying. Not only did he have serious problems of excessive self esteem, but he began to tell us about some weird series he was literally obsessed with! I gave Bailey's bagel and it was a little chewy, but it tasted better than I expected. There has always been a huge stereotype of school food being disgusting.

"So we´re settled for after school right?" Bailey asked when the bell rang.

"What? What for?" I asked startled.

"I´ll explain later *and* take that as a yes. Bye!" she said, and she ran off.

Oh god! I thought.

"So, what´s the plan?" I questioned on the bus.

"You´ll come over to my place and we can discuss book stuff. Sounds good?" she said.

"I´ve got homework," I said.

"That´s all right. We can do it together too."

There was a moment of silence.

"Well, okay," I finally said.

When I got home, I said, "Mom, I´m heading over to Bailey´s in a little while. Is that all right?" I said.

"Sure. You know, you and this Bailey are hanging out a lot. We should invite her some day, I´d love to meet her and get to know her better! She sounds wonderful!" she said drying her hands with a towel.

6

I rang the door bell on the yellow house. "*Who is it?*" Mrs. Gray's voice said through the speaker.

I stuttered, "Chase!"

"I'll be right there!" Mrs. Gray said.

I rearranged the books under my arm. Seconds later, the brown door opened.

"Chase! Hi! We are so glad to have you this afternoon!" Mrs. Gray said in an especially sweet and velvety voice.

"Thank you, Mrs. Gray," I said.

"Oh, please! Call me Janette!" she flattered. "Come on in!" she said moving aside to let me in.

"Thanks," I said.

She closed the door behind me. Mrs. Gray, or Janette, was tall, beautiful (so this is where Bailey got it from!), and she had sandy hair.

I glared at the house. It was amazing! On the right was a coat hanger where Janette demanded me to hang my jacket. She was as insistent as a goat, so I didn´t fight it and did as ordered. On my left was a living room with a flat screen TV, a long sofa, and a little coffee table. It was wide and spacious. In front of me was a staircase which welcomed you to go to the second floor.

"Bailey´s up-" Mrs. Gray was cut off by Bailey.

"I´m here, I´m here," Bailey said waving a hand as if to signal us not to worry.

"Oh, okay honey. I thought you were upstairs," Janette said.

"Well before I was, but now I´m here," she said. "Come on, Chase," she said holding out her hand, "It´s working time!"

She tugged me to her room. The moment we entered, she rushed to the window and took my books.

"What in god's name are you doing?" I asked.

She didn´t answer and pushed up the window. I saw her step on the rim and pop her whole body out of the window. She grabbed onto the roof and through my stuff onto the top of it.

"Are you a good climber?" she asked.

"Why?!" I asked incredulously.

"´Cause you´ll need it!" she said.

In a blink of an eye, Bailey jumped up on the roof and disappeared.

"Bails?!" I asked nervously.

Suddenly her head popped into the scene, upside down.

"I´m fine! Come on!" she said.

I advanced towards the window and put my foot on the rim. I imitated all the moves Bailey had done. Bailey´s hand was already extended towards me.

"Come on!"

I took it and I was lifted smoothly.

"Welcome to my working slash homework-doing place!" she said.

The neighborhood looked way too good from up here.

"Wow! Shall we get started?" I said.

"We shall," she said.

I shivered a bit and wanted to have my jacket with me. When we finished our homework with riddance, Bailey and I decided that we didn´t feel like doing book stuff.

"It´s amazing how you can see people, but people can´t see you from up here-well, unless they look up here really closely," Bailey said.

"Yeah. Hey, I have written like two more chapters!" I announced.

"Great! Hey, do you feel like doing book stuff now?" she asked.

"It´s weird, but I do!" I answered making a face.

"Okay, I say that once Peter is in Swordenslane Island, he can meet a fairy," Bailey suggested.

"Yeah! That would be cool! Her name could be- Tiffany! Do you like it?" I questioned.

"I love it!" she agreed.

We bickered like little airhead girls for two hours straight. It was dusk, and the sky was composed of a mix of orange and pink.

"You don´t get many pretty sunsets here, you know. We got a stroke of luck," I said.

"Yeah, we did get a stroke of luck; and I don´t only mean the sunset," she said.

I started to blush like I usually did with the slightest embarrassment.

"Your blushing gives you away, ALWAYS," she teased.

"Well your eyes give *you* away!" I replied.

She looked away, just in case her eyes could do anything else. She lay on her back, face up, and I followed. We just lay there, looking up at the sky in silence. It was hard not turn my head to the left, and look at her. But Bailey ended up surrendering before I did. She looked at me. When I discovered that, I pulled myself together and turned to look at her.

"I say we have a little fun today," I said, breaking the piercing silence.

"We haven´t had fun yet?" she asked amused.

"I´m not saying we haven´t, I´m saying we should have even more fun! Shall we dance?" I asked standing up giving my hand to her for support. Where was all this coming from? This is something I never did! I guess when I was with Bailey, I couldn´t be anyone else but myself.

She took my hand and stood up. "I kind of suck," she said making a nervous face.

"Well then that makes two of us," I said.

She laughed. I took her hand and waist, a little zap zooming up from my fingers to my elbow. She took my hand and my shoulder. We began slowly, until I picked up the pace. We were skipping like you would in a rodeo dance in different directions. We were both laughing hysterically, and I gave her little turns and such. When finished completely exhausted and with aching bellies we literally dropped to the floor, still laughing.

"You´re not so bad you know. Actually, you´re pretty good!" I said teasingly.

"You´re not so bad yourself," she reeled back, panting.

"It´s seven, I´ve got to go home now," I said looking at my watch.

"Okay, well let´s get back in," she said.

We climbed back down into Bailey´s room. I grabbed my stuff and headed down the stairs with Bailey right behind me.

"Did you kids have fun?" Mrs. Gray asked downstairs.

"Yes, yes we did Mrs. Gray, I mean, Janette," I said.

She smiled and opened the front door for me. I took my jacket, barely remembering I had it, and put it on.

"Bye!" Bailey and Janette said together.

"Bye, thank you," I said.

I slid my hands into my pockets, thinking dizzily about her. Those turns had given me the whiplash.

7

“We´re going to have to drop out Michael from the little league baseball,” My mom whispered. “We can´t afford it much longer,” she explained, “After this season he´s going to stop playing.”

“You know what? I´ll tell him mom,” I offered.

“What, are you kidding me? I´m his mother I´ll tell him!” she said.

“Mom, I´m his brother, and I understand him too,” I said.

“Okay, but don´t be too hard with it!” she begged.

“I won´t,” I assured.

I climbed up the stairs and knocked on Michael´s door.

“Come in!” Mike´s voice said.

I turned the doorknob and entered. Mike was about to make a little toy soldier fly with his car.

"What´s up, Chase?" he asked.

"Well, there´s something I have to tell you, buddy." I sucked in a deep breath and said, "You know, we´ve been having some trouble because our family´s budget is a little tight."

Mike just nodded and kept smiling happily.

"And this season- just imagine this okay? In a game, a player is going to bat, right?" I asked to make sure he understood.

"Mhmmm!" he responded.

"Well, this player has two strikes already and he only has one more chance. He hits it, but it´s the last time he´s going to play. And that player is you, Mike. Since we have to save up the money this is your last season. But that´s cool right? I mean, we can still play here," I explained.

"What do you mean? I´m not playing baseball anymore?"

Uh oh. "Well, you´ll stop playing with the little league but you´re not going stop playing forever. You can play with me, okay?"

"Okay, that´s cool," he said.

"All right. Well, see you later little man," I said, made a half hearted smile and left the room.

My mom was standing outside the room, and clearly, she had listened to everything. I made a face full of amusement.

"You heard everything didn´t you?" I asked.

"Oh, what did you expect? I couldn´t help it!"

We just started laughing a little. My mom pulled me into her chest and gave me a big hug. She kissed the top of my head, and said, "You know, when I married your father, I thought to myself, I want all girls, no boys. We never expected to have only boys, and the best of it all is, I don´t regret it one bit," she said. She kissed my head one more time, and let go.

I smiled in affection and said, "Thanks, mom."

"I think I´m up for some hot chocolate. ´You with me?" she said.

"Sure," I answered.

We sat in the tall chairs in the kitchen. My mom took out the chocolate powder and the milk.

"So how has school been?" my mom asked, mixing the milk and the chocolate together in both cups at the same time.

"Fine," I replied shortly.

"Can I get more than one word?" she said.

"It´s been okay," I answered.

She looked at me over her shoulder as she stuck the cups into the old microwave.

"That was three words!" I said raising my hands up as if to surrender.

She clicked the time in and the microwave started turning.

"Are your teachers nice?" she asked.

"Yes. Ms. Zelther´s great and well, Copmik- not so good," I said.

The microwave made it´s squeaky little *ding!* to signal that our beverages were ready. My mom stood up and opened the little door. She pulled out to steamy, green cups that smelled like heaven.

"Order´s up!" she said.

I took one and put it on the table. "Thanks. Ma, do you think someone can change another person?" I questioned.

"As in? Looks, attitude?" she said.

"I mean, can someone make you different? More confident? Maybe even happier?"

"Look, Chase," she said taking a sip out of her cup. "Anyone can change. Either voluntarily, or maybe the world changes them; and sometimes, it´s not the world. It might be one single person out there. As much as someone might be able to change you, it´s your choice to change because of that person, or not change at all," she explained.

I brushed the rim of my cup with my thumb, and took a cautious sip.

"And then, there´s other times were it´s not a choosing thing and that just changes you naturally," she added.

I lost my train of thought because I burned my tongue. "Ha co´ you dibn´t ge´ bur´?!" I squealed, my tongue out.

"Honey, I could be drinking boiling water and I wouldn´t get burned," my mom said.

I ended up dropping an ice cube into my drink as I thought about what my mother had said. Bailey´s image appeared in my head.

"What are you thinking about?" my mom asked.

I must have had a really concentrated expression. "Nothing, just blacked out for a second you know. My brain just- stopped."

We finished our treats and headed upstairs. *There´s other times where it´s not a choosing thing and that person just changes you naturally.*

The next day, when I entered my house, my mom´s first words were, "Mike´s last game is on Friday. You in?"

"Can Bailey come along?" I asked curiously.

"Sure, sure. She can come over before the game if you want," she suggested, popping a pill into her mouth and gradually swallowing it with a glass of water.

"Okay," I said.

The next morning in the bus I questioned Bailey, "Got plans for tomorrow?"

"No, why?" she asked.

"Tomorrow is my little brother´s last baseball game. Want to come?" I said.

"Great, okay!" Bailey answered.

Friday came quickly, and before I could even notice, Bailey was already being greeted by Mary and Ryan Russell. Bailey had a baseball cap with a California Dodgers logo.

"Hello, Bailey. How are you?" my mother said.

"Good, Mrs. Russell. Thank you for asking."

"Um, Chase has told me that you are working on a *book* together. Is that right?" my dad asked.

I looked at her to find the answer upon her expression, which revealed nothing.

She said firmly,"Yes, we are."

"Oh, okay. I see that you´re a Dodger fan," my father continued, pointing at her cap.

"Oh, no. Not really. I´m not much of a baseball fan so I just follow the teams my dad goes for," she explained.

My father´s mouth opened to say something, but no sound came out so instead he just closed his mouth and grinned. Suddenly, Michael appeared with his baseball outfit, a mit in his hand, and a hat on his head.

"I´m ready!" he said.

"Okay, lets go!" I said and I quickly stood up.

Bailey followed with my parents.

"Wait for me! Wa- wait!" Ben´s voice said behind us.

I turned around and there was my brother, panting and catching up. My siblings, Bailey and I climbed up onto the back of the Ford pick up, as my parents got into the front. The trees, houses and shrubs passed quickly beside us as we rode off.

When we finally got to the baseball field, we saw parents finding seats on the bleachers and boys warming up in the middle of the field. Their faces looked nervous and worried. But Michael wasn't. He had a confident look and his charming little smile on.

He hopped out of the back and said, "Mom, dad, I have to run! If not I'll be late!"

"Oh okay, honey. Good luck!" my mom said stumbeling out of her seat. She gave him a one armed hug and then Mike bolted off into the field. We made our way through the crowd to get a seat. A narrow space in between a fat man and a little old lady. We sat there, Ben having the seat next to the fat guy.

"Good morning, ladies and gentlemen. Today we have the final between the Mighty Hawks and the Wolves!" the host said over the loud speaker. Both coaches gave a thumbs-up, and the balding host said, "The Mighty Hawks bat first. Playball!"

Mike's team, The Wolves, went out and took the field. A boy in his purple Mighty Hawk uniform advanced to home plate. I looked for Mike shading my eyes from the sun.

"Look! There's Michael on second base!" Bailey said.

I turned my head to the left and there he was, my little brother. I cheered strongly and said,"Woo! Yeah, Mike!" as I clapped.

The first pitch came, and the boy at home plate swung the bat and hit the ball. It soared through the air towards my brother's glove. He got his mitt ready and-

"OUT!" the host announced.

The crowd cheered. Michael had the ball in his mitt, which he lifted as if to let the crowd see it.

"What a start, folks!" the host said, "Batter up!"

The game was more exciting than what I had expected. Then it was the Wolfes turn to bat. Some hit the ball, others were stricken out. The score was a tie. Nine to nine.

"Okay! Last batter up! This will define which team wins and loses. The last batter for the Wolves is-" he checked his list, "Michael Russell!"

All five of us stood up and pounded our fists in the air.

"Go, Michael!" Bailey said.

Mike was already standing at home plate. The Mighty Hawk pitcher threw the ball.

"Strike one!" the host said.

The whole crowd groaned. Second swing-

"STRIKE TWO!" the host said.

The crowd groaned even louder. This was trully nerve wrecking. *Last one, Michael!* I thought. The pitcher threw the last ball and-

"Woohoo!" the crowd cheer.

Mike´s ball was high in the air while he flew through the bases. The Mighty Hawks were flustered.

"This has got to be a home run! Will it be? Is it?" the host said suspenfully. Michael slid in successfully and-"Yes! The Wolves win!"

The team with the boys in red uniforms cheered along with the crowd. Mike's coach swooped him up into his shoulders, making him look ten feet tall. We rushed down the bleachers, my mom saying,"That's my boy! That's my Mikey!" Even my hostile brother Ben was going crazy. We celebrated with hotdogs. When we finished eating, Bailey and I took a stroll along the wirefence.

"That was so much fun!" Bailey said wrapping her fingers around the chain links.

"Yeah, Mike was good. I'm glad he won; it's his last time with the Little Legue, so he deserves it," I said.

Bailey turned around, her back resting on the fence. She sighed and looked at me.

"I wish I had a brother. I've got one sister and she is more than enough!" she explained rolling her eyes.

"Wait-you have a sister?" I asked her.

"Yeah! Her name is Emma," she explained.

"How old is she?"

"She's turning sixteen in a week or so," she explained.

My jaw fell open. "What?" Bailey asked.

"We have too much in common!" I said, thinking about Ben. "Is Emma pretty?" I questioned.

She laughed,"Yeah, you could say that," she said.

"My brother is such a teenager! He is stuck in the narrow tube of puberty," I admitted.

"Sounds like a replica of my sister."

"We should hook them up!" I said.

"Huh?"

"Who knows? Maybe they like each other!" I suggested.

"Mmmm- maybe," she finished.

"You know what?" I said while putting my arm over her shoulder.

"What?" she asked copying my move.

I stepped on her foot, almost tripping her.

"Aah!" she gasped hysterically as she stepped on my foot.

We started battling from left to right, stomping and tripping each other. I put my foot over Bailey´s, this time tripping her succesfully, making her collapse where we were. She accidentally brought me down with her, the result being me falling too. I hit the ground as hard as I was laughing. As we both stumbled to our feet, giggling uncontrolably and trying gasping for breath, my family appeared.

"Going back home, kids!" my mom said.

We both quieted down. Bailey wiped a strand of hair off her face.

"Okay, Mom. Right behind you!" I said.

My father turned on his heel followed by the rest of us in the direction of the parking lot. Me and Bailey looked at each other and burst into snickers. We were literally bending in half. With undetermined cordination we both sighed, straightened up, and reached the car in total silence.

The ride home was silent, except for Bailey talking to Ben. Their conversation was silent, almost whispered as if it were a deep and magical secret no one could know. We arrived at Bailey´s quickly, in what felt like seconds. Both Bailey and I jumped out of the back.

"Bailey, it was very nice having you with us today, I hope you come around soon.," my father said grinning.

"Thank you, Ryan. I had a very good time!" Bailey answered, shaking his hand.

It was weird how my dad did that with absolutely everyone. From the old plumber to Uncle Max.

"Bailey, sweetheart, let´s see you soon allright? Come on, let´s get you back home," mom said putting a hand on her back, guiding her back to the door on the yellow house. Bailey´s mom opened the door.

"Oh, hello! I´m Janette, and you must be-"

"Mary," my mother finished for her.

"Mary, thank you so much for bringing Bailey home. I was really busy today. I´m a lawyer so," Janette explained.

"Oh, that´s great! Well, we will see you soon. Goodbye!" mom said.

"Goodbye, Mary- and Chase," Janette said as she closed the door.

"Well, her mother is very nice," my mom said smiling.

I barely noticed walking back to the truck that my fahter had stayed next to the pick up the whole time.

"Let's go back home," my father affirmed and he walked to the door on the driver´s seat. While we were riding home I shivered, winter was definetely on it´s way.

DECEMBER

"Honey, put your scarf on, would you?" my mother said on Friday morning, the last day of school before winter holidays. I did as requested. "I don´t want you to get sick the day before break."

"I always have and I always will get sick, it´s inevitable!" I said.

My mother chuckled and put her hands on my shoulders. "Run to the bus stop or you will be late!"

"Okay, mom, Bye!" I said and I kissed her cheek.

At the bus stop I folded my arms to warm myself up. The girl next to me was a small first grader that was stomping her feet on the slightly thick snow sheet under us.

"I- I'm fr- freezing!" she chattered.

"If you don´t think about it, you´ll be less cold. You will be physically cold but not psychologically. And that reduces the cold because sixty percent of your cold is psychological so that leaves only forty percent of the cold. You get me?" I asked.

The little girl stared at me with a "say-what?" face.

"Okay, never mind that," I told her.

Her expression did not change. The bus arrived with the squeaky sound of its tires on the pavement. We climbed up the stairs quickly. It made no difference to be outside or on the bus, it was equally cold. The bus´s heater was clearly wrecked.

We approached the yellow house, which lifted my spirits up a little. As Bailey walked forward she looked wonderful. For some reason she blushed, and for the first time she had color upon her face.

"Oh my god! What is up with the weather?!" she said.

"Welcome to Ohio!" I said. She nudged me lightly with her elbow. We were silent for a couple of minutes, constantly shivering. "Why do I feel like I´m in prison?" I asked. She laughed.

The building was much warmer. Even Mrs. Meredith Stein´s class was comforting, which is quite unusual.

There was a really stupid "Holiday Assembly." Four shy eighth grade girls were supposed to do a "musical and vocal" performance…Yeah right! I think listening to Barney´s Hit Parade would have been a treat compared to the girls´ show. The Principal dressed up as Santa Claus and did the whole *Ho ho ho! Merry Christmas!* thing. It was a pretty funny thing to see Principal Callaway do it. The rest was pretty good…for a school assembly.

"What are you doing for the holidays?" Bailey asked as we left the building.

"Staying home, as usual," I honestly answered.

"Me too, well, first I´m going visit Papu and then come back. He´s not far away though, and we´ll only visit one day." I looked at her in a who-the-heck-is-Papu? way. "He´s my grandfather," She explained.

"Mom or dad´s side?" I said.

"Mom´s. My grandpa on my father´s side died a couple of years ago," she said.

"I´m sorry about that," I said.

"I didn´t get to see him a lot so it wasn´t that hard for me. But if Papu- left, it would be really tough. We´re two peas in a pod!" she said.

"I´ve never had anyone in my family or friends die. I haven´t been to a funeral either," I corresponded.

"I have only been to grandpa Joe´s. It was only one, but it was more than enough."

"If you die, you´re going to heaven which is paradise, so then dying sounds like a good way to go, doesn´t it?" I wondered.

"Well, yeah but don´t you want to live?" Bailey asked.

"Of course I want to live! Almost everybody does. I mean we´re all afraid of dying, right?" I stated.

"I´m not," she said casually.

"Really? You are not?" I said in disbelief.

"Yeah, what I´m afraid of is when it will happen. You know it´s going to happen and it´s inevitable, but you don′t know when it′ll catch by surprise. Not that I want to know."

"Okay, this is bad conversation, let′s change the subject," I suggested.

"Good idea," she chuckled.

The bus stopped violently and we all rocked forward and back, some girls screaming. Everybody dismounted the bus, but Bailey and I were the last ones. I went down the stairs first. "Madam," I said extending my hand for support.

"Don′t mind if I do!" Bailey said taking my hand and skipping off the last step.

We walked towards the school. I looked up at the crooked Winesburg Middle School sign, "That sign is so old and rusty. I swear some day that M in Middle is going to fall, don′t you think?" I said looking to my left, searching for Bailey. "Bails?" I asked. She had disappeared. "Hey, where′d you go?" I said. I looked at the right, and under a tree was Jeremy Hirsch messing with Bailey. She kept squealing things like, "Let go!" and, "Stop! Don′t touch me!"

"Hey, hey! Don′t worry about it. I just ran into you," Jeremy said.

"*Ran into me?* Something pulled my hand so hard and suddenly I was right next to you, idiot!" Bailey said more seriously now.

"You seem to be mistaken. My name is not Idiot, it′s Jeremy Isaac Hirsch, nice and Jewish," he explained.

"Well Jeremy Isaac Hirsch, not very nice to meet you! Goodbye!" Bailey said slapping his arm with the back of her hand.

"Oh, come on!" Jeremy taunted, standing in front of her.

I found myself walking towards them, both of my hands balled up into fists. *Calm down,* I thought to myself. *Handle this the right way.* I relaxed my hands and neck, lowering my accelerated pace. I reached them. "Hello, Jeremy," I said in a sarcastically friendly tone. "You seem quite confused on where you´re going. You´re obviously mistaken," I continued.

"I´d say I´m just fine where I am, birdbrain!" he said.

"Hey! Kick it down a notch, will you?!" Bailey exclaimed harshly.

Jeremy released her and snarled. Bailey gave him a hateful look and walked in the school´s direction.

"By the way, Hirsch, you suck at hitting on girls. Word of advice, don´t uses this one again," I said and turned around.

I expected a brutal attack from him but Jeremy didn´t even respond. I rushed up to Bailey. "Are you okay?" I asked as I stopped her with my hand.

"I´m fine, I don´t want to talk about it," she said.

"Bails, he was really out there. I mean-" I was stopped by her pained expression.

"Just- just let it go," she finalized, and walked away.

I just stood there- useless- feeling like an old and forgotten rag doll on a shelf.

I heard the bell ring as I started to leave my desk. I went to my locker and started putting in the combination. I opened the little door.

"Knock knock!" a familiar voice said gently hitting the door. I didn´t answer and put my books inside. "Look, are you still really upset and mad about this morning? It was just that I was really pissed off and-"

"It's fine," I answered shortly.

"Aren´t you- mad?" Bailey asked.

For the first time I looked up at her. She looked preoccupied. "I mean, I was also pissed off, you know. Not with you though, with Jeremy," I said straightening up. Whoops! I let it slip!

"So you were worried about me?" she questioned almost smiling.

I quickly replied, "You have no idea what Hirsch has done and can do!"

She half smiled while closing my locker with her foot.

"Thanks."

"You´re welcome. Hey do you- mind?" she said first pointing at her watch, then at the stairs.

No it´s fine. Who are you meeting?"

"Just MaryAnn and them. I´ll see you on the bus!" she said.

"Okay, see you," I replied.

I decided I could meet my guys, which narrowed down to Charlie, because the rest had "other plans." Who knows what that meant!

"It´s cold out!" Charlie said.

"Yeah, what´d you expect?" I said slightly sarcastically.

"Eh, you´re right," he answered. "It´s worse than planet Moro," he continued absent mindedly.

Pardon?" I asked lifting an eyebrow.

"You see, in Star Galaxy this T.V. show there´s this planet called Moro. That´s where Tarame the evil corgey lives! And the good guy from planet Splodakus, Wortado the marmod is trying to destroy Tarame with his college, Jaba," he began explaining, "But in last night´s episode- oh, man it was so cool!- Jaba betrayed Wortado! And-" he kept on going, until it was unbearable and I had to stop him.

"Okay! That sounds interesting, but I really have to go. Bye, Charlie!" I said as an excuse, starting to walk towards my bus.

"You should watch the marathon tonight on channel seven!" he shouted at me from a distance.

"Uh- all right! I´ll- do that!" I shouted back. "*Not,*" I whispered under my breath.

I let out a long sigh as I sat down in my seat. "Do you like Charlie?" I asked Bailey.

"I guess. Charlie's nice, why not?" she inquired.

"He just gave me a lecture on this weird like, space T.V. program," I said shivering.

"What´s it called?" she asked.

"Star Galaxy or something. God it´s frightening! Television is eating children! How´d it go for you?" I said.

She laughed and answered, "Better than you, obviously. Isabella is slightly stupid- sometimes," she said, "Didn´t you hear her comment at lunch today?" she asked.

"Apparently not," I answered.

"She asked ´What is the country under the United States? ´" Bailey quoted with disbelief.

I didn´t say anything.

"Mexico!" she snapped.

"I know that!" I stuttered.

"God, I´m just tired. I´m going to take a nap until we get to my house," she said getting comfortable.

"Sweet dreams," I said.

"Don´t bet on it," she responded.

I laughed a little. She was asleep in seconds, tired and broken. Her head was bobbling on her left side so she looked kind of funny. Then in one of the buses bumps her head bopped in the opposite direction and landed on my shoulder with a little snore. She did not wake up. I did not move her head in the fear of waking her, it was too heavy anyway. So I decided to sleep too.

It felt like seconds later when I was brutally woken by a thud; it was my stop. Bailey woke up as well. “Oh, god! I´m out! See you when I see you, Bails! Have a nice vacation!” I said, and stumbled out of the bus.

8

"Huh?" I muttered. The first thing I saw when I opened my eyes in bed was my bed light, then the white ceiling, and then Mike's face staring at me as I rolled over to the right. His eyes were wide and his jaw was open.

"Chase, are you dead?!" He asked.

"No! What time is it?" I groaned, trying to straighten up. This attempt was failed.

"Your alarm clock says twelve thirty!" I sat up a little too quickly, my head spinning. I rubbed my eyes.

"Chase, what happened to you?" he asked, worried.

"I was tired, I slept late. We're on vacations now!" I said coughing right after, "Oh no! The sickness has caught up with my unworthy soul!" I said in a British accent, making my brother giggle.

"Okay, see you downstairs for breakfast, I mean *lunch,*" he emphasized.

He opened the door and left the room. *Oh god,* I thought reaching out for my alarm clock. I saw time pass by. "All right, get up," I told myself. Instead of doing as I suggested, I flopped back onto the bed.

Suddenly, the little thinking light bulb light up above my head. I should write. I went downstairs and found my family at the kitchen table, dressed, and setting the table for lunch.

"Good morning, honey. Do you want something for breakfast?" she asked, her tone a bit taunting.

"Morning everyone! No, mom. I believe that is no longer an option," I joked.

"Well then will you join us for lunch?"she said.

I groaned as I saw my writing time slip by, "I guess it wouldn´t hurt."

All through the meal I was anxiously waiting for the opportunity to slide out of my chair and dash up to my room. When everyone was done, I finally exhaled and said, "Well, I´m going to go write so, I´ll see you guys later! Thanks for the food ma, it was great!" I started climbing the stairs.

"Okay," my mother said below. Once I started writing, I reached page one hundred. Then I passed it, quick. Time slurred by silently as I kept on writing in my green, plaid pajamas, my hand soar.

137

"Tiffany, I´m not sure about all this! I´m not sure if I´m dead, dreaming, or if it´s simply- real," Peter finished.

"So you don´t believe that I´m real. You think I´m an illusion or a dream right?" Tiffany said.

"No! I mean, I want you to exist but I´m not sure if you do," he attempted to explain.

"Maybe you just have to believe," she suggested.

"That doesn´t prove it," Peter said stirring.

"Well, I´m not the only one. Corggle is a goblin, a fantastic creature just like me," the fairy said.

"Whoa, whoa! Who said my name?" Corggle´s voice complained as he materialized out of a bush. He ran in his funny way all the way to the water´s edge where Tiffany and Peter sat.

Peter played around with a pebble stuck in the sand. He stopped his actions, wrapped his arms around his legs, and rested his chin on his knees. Tiffany flittered over to his shoulder and stood on it, landing gently. Corggle finally reached them, panting.

"Who´s the criminal that dared to speak my name?" he said in a harassing tone. He shaped his fingers into a gun and pointed it at them.

"Nothing you have to kill for, Corggle," Tiff said.

Peter giggled under his breath.

"Oh well," the goblin said stretching up from his position. "So what are we going to do with the slight problem that this kid is miles away from his house?" Corggle asked waving his hand at Peter.

"Gee, Corggle! You´re really helpful right now!" Tiffany said sarcastically.

"No, Tiff. It´s not that I want to leave, because I love you guys, but that *is* a problem. My parents' heads are probably exploding! It must be mind boggling!" the boy said.

"Peter, honey, I hadn´t met anyone in three hundred years and then you came along," Tiffany explained.

"So that´s how old you are! Woo hoo! Finally!" Corggle interrupted as he pounded the air in victory.

Tiffany raised one eyebrow and put a hand on her waist. She shot a warning look at the laughing creature.

"Sorry!" he said clapping his hands over his mouth.

"You woke us all up! We were bored to our cores with our isolation. Thank god for those currents that pulled you here!" she exclaimed.

So that topic I wanted to cover was done. Now what? My hand stopped. I tried to keep writing, which I did, but it didn´t come out naturally. It was like the words I wrote were forced, and trying to be too good.

I returned to the real world for a second and I heard my mother downstairs: *I finished my book last night. I think there's nothing in this house I haven't read already!* She said.

That's not true, you're missing one manuscript I thought, *mine.*

I stood up and went to the door. I opened it and said, "Mom! I've got something for you!"

My mother brushed my writing with her fingertips, stroking it and smiling.

"Honey, is this your work?" she asked incredulously.

"Yeah," I answered shortly. "It's short so you'll finish it in no time," I teased.

"Hmmm, this is the best thing I can read right now. Thanks," she ruffled my hair.

Her fingers moved smoothly through my scalp.

"Sweetie, your hair is so soft! What shampoo are you using?" she said.

"Same as always, I just got the goods!" I joked.

She was going to say something, but then she thought twice. She tilted her head, studying me. She left the room speechless with my writing embraced in her arms.

That night I heard my mother crying, and I couldn't help the anxiety of knowing why. Her door was ajar, but I could see her in her bed curled up into a ball, reading. She pulled a Kleenex out of its box and blew really hard. She was probably in the emotional part where Peter goes into the ocean, followed by the strong currents that pull him away and his parents don't know what happened to him. I guess losing your child was a big deal. How couldn´t it be?

But I was happy then. I was glad to see that the emotion in the plot reached out and touched your heart- my mother´s heart. Well, she´s a sucker for emotional movies, writing, and pretty much everything!

I went back to bed, the corners of my lips pulled up all the way to my eyes.

December twentieth, I thought. Christmas was near. I had family reunions, all filled with comforting foods and the joyous company of our family members.

On a Monday morning, I got a call from Bailey. She offered an invitation to meet Papu. I asked my parents for permission and luckily, I got a yes. On Tuesday, I climbed into the Gray´s BMW. Before I closed the door on the door my mom said, "Chase?" from the front step of my house. When I looked at her, she signaled me to go to her with her index finger. I jumped out of the seat and shuffled forward towards my mother.

"Honey, um, have fun!" she said.

"Thanks, ma. I´ll see you later," I said impatiently. I turned around but she took my shoulder with one hand, and spun me around.

"Honey, your manuscript is- amazing. It´s like seriously professional writing!" she chuckled.

"Thanks, mom. But they´re kind of waiting for me, and-!" I said pointing at the car.

Malcolm, Bailey's father, smiled and nodded.

"Okay, see you later darling!" she said as I ran to the car.

During the drive, Bailey's hand was resting calmly in the space between us. I hadn't noticed this, so I accidentally moved my hand over hers. My stomach flipped over. But she did not recoil or pull away. It stood there, delicate, soft, and cold to my touch. She glanced at me with a happy smile and then looked away. My hand's heat must have been comforting to her. We did not move since we were both kind of tense.

That was until we reached a stop. "Where's- Emma?" I asked. I noticed that Bailey's sister was not with us. She looked surprised that I had remembered her name.

"She said she didn't want to waste her time on visits," Bailey answered.

We reached the front step and Malcolm knocked on the door. I didn't know what to expect. Bailey looked anxious and excited. The door opened and I saw a very bald man with white hair-in the scarce places he had it- a mustache, wrinkles, and spectacles.

"Papu!"Bailey exclaimed and threw herself on him.

Papu stumbled back a bit by the impact. He wrapped his arms around her.

"Oh, hello pumpkin!" he responded.

He put her down and kissed the top of her head. For a second I wished I were Papu.

Janette said smiling, "Hey pops!"

"Janny!" he said giving her a hug.

Now both Mrs. Gray and Bailey were inside.

"Malcolm."

"Sir," they shook hands in a friendly and close way.

"And who is this handsome, young man?" Papu asked.

Color brewed up on Bailey's cheeks at the word handsome. I was awfully pleased by this and grinned.

"Albert, this is Chase. He's Bailey friend," Malcolm introduced me.

"Hello, sir. Merry Christmas!" I added.

"Merry Christmas to you too! Please do come in, Chase!" Papu said.

I walked into the house, and it was very different than what I thought. There were things like fish carved out of wood hung on the wall, souvenirs from faraway places on shelves, and family pictures in frames.

"Please! Right around here!"Albert signaled me to the living room.

The others already knew where it was. We sat down in large, brown sofas.

"So um-" Papu started to talk to me.

"Chase," I reminded him my name.

"Right, I knew that. So, Chase, how did you meet my little Bailey?"

"Well, we go to the same school and we live in the same neighborhood now," I began.

"Very nice! And tell me Chase, why would you ever come visit this old man in the middle of Christmas holiday?"

"Excellent question, Albert. I actually have no idea!" with this I was saying the truth.

Everybody laughed.

"Chase and I have been working on a book together, Papu," Bailey added.

"Oh really? What have you been reading?" he asked unknowingly.

"No, Papu! We haven´t been reading. We have been writing! Well, Chase has. I just do the illustrations," she explained.

"Good heavens! You´re writing a book?" Papu turned to me incredulously.

I simply nodded.

"Oh and, Papu, you have got to tell Chase all your stories!"Bailey suggested.

"Now hold up, pumpkin!" Papu said.

"Chase, would you like to hear these boring stories from this old man?"Papu asked.

"Oh come on, Albert!" said Malcolm.

"Dad your stories are not boring!"Janette insisted.

"Well fine! Which one do you want to hear?" he asked convinced.

"All of them!" Bailey proposed.

So Papu started, "Well it all began when I retired from being a lawyer. I started to travel. So the first place I went to was New York," he explained.

Wow, I thought.

"So I did the touristic things. Central Park, Time Square, Statue of Liberty. I was thrilled by this city! At night all the lights would shine brightly. Broadway productions were out of this world!" he recalled, "The next place I went to was Mexico! Such rich culture! The food was truly spectacular. Tortillas, *chili* -as they call it there- beans, and you´d be surprised how much lime they use. They put it on everything! Even fruit! There were also flaming red tomatoes, tacos, pyramids, beaches, and best of all Mexican mariachis!"

Bailey was watching my reaction from the corner of her eye, which was my jaw dropped all the way to the floor.

Albert told us stories about South America, the rich variety of flora and fauna. When he talked about Alaska, the most popular words used were cold and ice. Then we traveled to Europe. He talked about the Eifel Tower, Italy, especially Venice. He described the *gondolieri* and their little boats in this beautiful and mysterious city. Then we went east, to Asia.

"India was twisted in two vines. Religion and truly humorous disorder! China was mind blowing. The Chinese wall was tall and majestic! Then I went to Russia. I got to see Saint Basil's which was gorgeous!" Papu continued.

He told us about how Ivan IV the first Russian czar which meant "little father" had asked the best architect in Russia to build him the most beautiful cathedral in the world and that was finally Saint Basil's.

With every place came a different story. Some were like Indiana Jones and others like Peter Pan- Surreal. The final places were Sweden, Australia, New Zealand, Egypt, and Turkey. As if they weren't enough already! But my favorite story was the one that took place in Santorini, Greece.

"I arrived to the deck on a small boat. I caught the smell of donkey poop!" We all chuckled a bit. "So it turned out that a donkey was exactly what I rode up on to get to the village. It was a zigzag road and the donkeys were like programmed robots! When there was a beautiful landscape or angle of the ocean it stopped, let you take a picture, and then it took off again. While you were riding up, huge flocks of around thirty donkeys came running right at you! Nothing happened to me but it was a close call! The village was beautiful. The houses were white, their dome ceilings painted royal blue. Other houses were soft pastel colors. I started to wonder around the souvenir stores when I saw this beautiful bottle of Ouzo. It took me about 20 minutes to be able to communicate with the guy from the store and finally purchase the bottle. When I tried it, it hit me like a bombshell! It was the strongest liquor I had ever tried! Took me like six months to wash it down. I didn't want to waste it. And I still have the bottle!" Papu remarked.

He stood up and walked to a shelf close by, and there it was; the famous bottle of Ouzo. He took it in his wrinkled hands, and brought it back. I was the first to be able to see the bottle. It was all in Greek. Still, it looked amazing!

Papu and the rest of us kept talking, time unnoticed. Papu turned out to be a very fun grandfather! I checked the watch wrapped around my wrist. We had arrived at 10:30 in the morning and it was five o´clock already! It felt like we had just eaten lunch, and soon it would be time for dinner! I guess I was too amazed by the stories that swept me off my feet, and now it all came together and I found the pieces to the puzzle. Now I understood why Bailey adored Papu and why he was so important to her. She probably got her drawings out of her imagination flowing through his stories. This visit in which I was only supposed to meet an old man turned out to be a blizzard storm of ideas that were now swirling through my mind.

We said goodbye and left on the BMW. We (Bailey and I) could not stop talking on the way back.

"Look, how does this sound? When they're trying to find a way back for Peter, they get lost. It turns out that the island has different landscapes depending on which direction you move!" I suggested.

"Yeah, that sounds great. How about in Swordenslane Island, north is east, east is south, and south is west is north! Like they change clockwise," she said.

"Okay, so let´s pick places. I say they should be like different climates or regions. For example, jungle can be-" I thought.

"South America! Brazil, maybe. God, Papu´s a genius!" Bailey remarked.

"For a desert we can use Egypt!"

Then we decided we would use Alaska for cold. And Santorini type for ocean site.

When they leave Swordenslane forest, they will hit the Santorini-ish landscape. Corggle will find a bottle of Ouzo, drinks it, and accidentally becomes drunk. Then in the desert, they will find an oasis in which they will fall into. Cruising through a water geyser they would be squirted out to the jungle. We didn´t exactly know how they would get from the jungle to the icy land, but Peter would return home in companionship of Corggle and Tiffany. Once he leaves he would obviously be sad but would never forget the adventures he had had with his friends. Many things will happen in the different areas apart from the changing to the next one. Maybe things like exploding volcanoes, making rafts, and campfires! I wanted pure adventure.

As we were talking, the car stopped in front of my house. I said thank you and goodbye as I ran towards the door.

9

December twenty fourth! Now I thought. The day before Christmas. I poured orange juice into my glass, and my mom had made little gingerbread cookies. It was barely morning, and she was already preparing the turkey, the stuffing, and basically the entire dinner. It would be Christmas Eve, the tree shining bright. The doorbell rang and I was the closest to the door, so I got it. I opened the door, and nobody was there. I looked around trying to find somebody. I glared down at my feet and I saw a yellow envelope-like package. I took it in my hands and flipped it over. All it said was DRAWINGS, in big block capital letters. *Bailey.*

After breakfast I flew to my room and opened the letter anxiously. The first thing I found was a letter written in Bailey´s handwriting:

Dear Chase,

Merry Christmas! I hope you have the most wonderful holidays! This is a little present/due

work for you. I hope you like them as much as I had fun drawing them. Happy holidays again.
Love,

Bailey.

P.S. We need a book publisher! SOS!!!

I reread over and over again the word love. Did she feel the same way about me as I felt about her? I got the feeling that I was about to pee myself. But then I snapped out of it, and moved on to the drawings. There were loads of them! There were pictures of the geyser, the oasis, the volcano, and my personal favorite, a drunk Corggle with a bottle of Ouzo in his hand.

I never got tired of Bailey's drawings. How could I? They were too spectacular. I read the last part again. *We need a publisher!* In that instant I started shuffling through every shelf to find books that I liked. I dug under every place possible. When I found one of my favorites, I flipped it to look at the spine. "Wrightman Books, perfect!" I said to myself.

I went downstairs to the old PC. I turned it on, getting ready for the waiting time. After ten minutes, I was finally connected to the internet. I did not know the URL or website of this publisher-if they had one- so I typed *www. wrightmanbooks.com,* nice and simple. I clicked enter and waited. After a little while, the website appeared. My heart leaped. I read some of the important things like what type of company they were and what they wanted to accomplish for you. When I read that to submit your work it had to be typed, I immediately opened a document and ran upstairs for my notebook. Once I was back I started right away, and my mother helped me edit it to make it final.

I had to tell Bailey about our new progress. I picked up the phone and dialed her number.

"Hello?" Bailey's voice said through the phone.

"Hey, Bails! Merry Christmas!" I said.

She laughed, "Thanks, you too! So, did you get the package?"

"Yes, thank you so much. And guess what? We have a publisher!" I announced.

"No way! Which one?" said Bailey.

"Wrightman Books! It looks great!"

"That's the best news I've heard all day, Chase! You saved us! Well, Merry Christmas! Bye," she said.

"Bye," I hung up and thought, *Oh, and by the way, I really like you and I think I just might have fallen in love with you. Ugh Chase, you're being lame!* The voice inside my head told me. *Shut up!* I told him.

"Santa's here!" Mike exclaimed in the morning. We all went downstairs to open the presents under the Christmas tree. I got a dipping ink pen, a sweatshirt, a pair of amazing sneakers, and two CD's that I had been dying to have. I listened to them all day. My mom made a special Christmas breakfast. We had pancakes shaped into presents, trees, and holiday decorations. We also each got a glorious cup of her tasty cocoa. It was truly a great Christmas.

DECEMBER 28

The phone rang early in the morning and I picked it up. "Yellow," I joked. On the other side of the phone I heard heavy sobbing.

"Chase?" the familiar voice I loved croaked.

I started to panic as chaos came over me, "Bailey? Bailey what´s wrong?"

She sniffled and choked out the words; "Papu- died!" she broke into hard sobs again.

This was like one of my terrible nightmares. My feet were stuck and I couldn´t run away. "Oh god! When-how?" I asked.

She sucked in a deep breath and said, "Last night. I think it was a heart attack," she explained.

The best I could do was gasp.

"I-" sniffle, "I called because the funeral is today at noon. I was wondering if you wanted to go," she said.

"Bails, I barely knew him! I only met him once!"

"But it was a heck of a meeting don´t you think?"

I hesitated for a moment, "Well yeah, but-"

"Please, Chase," she cried, "do it for me."

When I told my mother the news, she was awestruck, "Chase, I think you should go." She hugged herself and shivered.

I buttoned down my white shirt, folded the collar, and tucked it into my pants. I sighed. My mom opened the door.

"Chase, it's time to go."

When we arrived, I saw an image that I only imagined or had seen in films. People dressed in black, crying, a priest, and the coffin; Papu's coffin. My mom kissed me goodbye, and shuffled back to the car.

I walked forward to the crowd, making my way through it. I searched the faces, every single one of them miserable, until I found the one I was looking for. Bailey wore a black dress with some thick tights. The snow was falling, and the cold was present. Her face was paler than ever, and her eyes had never been so piercing.

"Chase!" said Bailey, and she walked towards me.

Malcolm and Janette appeared seconds later. Malcolm put a hand over Bailey's shoulder, gesturing that it was time. She took my hand and softly pulled me to the front with her. The priest appeared from the crowd. So the ceremony began.

"In the name of the Father, the Son, and the Holy Spirit-" the priest said.

Through the lectures, Janette held Bailey in a tight embrace, trying not to cry as much as she was. After all, Papu was her father. I tried to picture losing my father, but it was too painful. Malcolm cautiously put a strong arm around my shoulders. I looked up at him, he gave me a half hearted smile, and then his glance moved to the icy ground.

Minutes later, his arm flopped down, and he hobbled over to Janette. She instantly released Bailey and collapsed onto Malcolm. She let out quiet sobs, trying to breathe.

Bailey was left dangling. Then, I walked to her, and she repeated the actions of her mother. She buried her face in my chest. I put an arm around her and held her head with the other hand.

She cried as the priest said, "Albert was a wonderful man. He cared for others as a lawyer, and he cherished the world with his incessant travel."

It sounded terrifying how he talked about Papu in a past tense. And as much as he kept saying he was in a better place, it felt like he was gone- forever. I nervously and gently rested my cheek on top of Bailey blonde hair. I dropped my second hand and finished off the hug.

"Now, I ask for a moment of silence in honor of this outstanding man, brothers and sisters."

Then, it felt like the world and the ones around us shut down, and disappeared into nothingness. And with a trembling voice I whispered, "Don´t worry about it. Imagine how happy he is right now." She sniffled a little. "Imagine what a great time he´s having, and we´re here crying about that; we shouldn´t be. Don´t worry."

I started weaving my fingers through her hair in a comforting mode. It was silky, like my mom´s old prom dress she kept in a box. Holding her so close like that, it was an electric field. There were constant little zaps that were like reality checks of what was really happening. I heard the priest say, "In the name of the Father, the Son, and the Holy Spirit, Amen." That was when both Bailey and I instantly dropped our arms and broke apart. People looked back up. I guess we both knew that. Then some people put some flowers on the coffin. Janette pulled out the bottle of Ouzo and put it on top, too. Bailey did not move. Not an inch. She just stood there as a glistening tear rolled down per pale cheek.

"Time is ruthless isn´t it?" Bailey said looking up at me with a wounded expression.

My throat tightened, "Yes, yes it is."

When it was time, my mother came down the street sluggishly. I said goodbye to Bailey and her parents. I gave her one last hug, and ran back to the car. The vehicle moved forward, as I left with a heavy heart.

***

I was running, wheezing, through a black tunnel. Suddenly, there was a light post in the distance of the strange space. I looked over my shoulder, and there was nothing. I heard a wail in the distance that was calling for help, so I ran to it. I drowned in light again, as I turned the corner.

I stopped when I felt that heat and caught the smell of burning plywood. Those colorful flames were dancing before me- That´s when I woke up. I was panting and sweating. My chest inflated as I desperately inhaled for air. I looked around the room. Everything was in its place, my desk still inexplicably clean. The clock that was hung on the wall ticked on a steady beat, which made everything much worse and annoying.

I took a look at the time, trying to avoid its vague noise. *10:30?* I thought. It was true. I went to bed early since the funeral had kicked me hard in the stomach, so when I came back and flopped onto the bed I grew unconscious in seconds. Being there so deeply asleep, it was falling into nothingness. Just there, until my feet hit the black pavement and the running began.

The next couple of days, Bailey was really in that grief cycle thing. At first she was in deep shock. Her eyes were wide and expressionless, and it seemed like she had lost all power of speech. Then came denial, where she would just shake her head in disagreement whenever the topic of Papu came up. Avoidance trickled along when she ate compulsively and non-stop. The stage of anger didn´t last long, fortunately. The few days it occurred she just burst of rage about anything as easily as a bubble. When she was finally rolling into the last step, acceptance, I decided to go visit her.

I stepped forward and knocked on the door.

"Come in," Bailey´s voice came from inside.

All though it was already eleven, Bailey remained lying on her bed wearing a nicely fitting, grey t-shirt. I pulled the chair near her desk up to where she was. "Hi," I said.

"Hey," she said rolling over to face me.

She pulled out her arm and supported per head on her pale hand, as her elbow pressed down on the pillow. She smiled. “So, how′ve you been?”

“Much better actually! It has only been a week. How′ve you been?” she wondered.

“I′m fine,” I answered shortly.

She still looked sleepy but was attentive to our conversation, “I slept really late last night.”

“Why?” I questioned.

“Just thinking,” she continued.

“′Bout what?”

“Sounds cheesy, but life,” she blushed.

“Do go on,” I encouraged.

“I wonder how you live up to it,” she said.

“Maybe just by living and being the best you can be,” I suggested queerly.

“No offense but, that sounds kind of cheesy too,” she laughed, “Yet it makes sense,” she continued.

“Touché!” I said pointing at her.

I noticed that I still had a hard time talking to her, not as much as before, but I still thought about what to say, do, or how to act. *I wish I could borrow a girl′s brain for a while, see how they think,* I thought to myself.

“Hey, I was thinking,” she began.

I snapped back to attention.

"We should, um, show the manuscript to Mrs. Nacker, and see what she thinks," her expression was patient.

"What for?" I asked.

"I think she′d like to see it," she said.

"Maybe we should," I said giving it little thought. I glanced over to one of her crammed shelves and saw a collection of Smuckers Jelly jars that were overflowing with little coins. "What in the world are those for?" I asked.

"When I was a little girl I saved them for a rainy day," she explained.

"I cannot think of any useful way to use those," I said.

We both laughed as she playfully slapped my head in a gentle and friendly way. I purposefully hung my head down.

"Sometimes I count ′em up when I′m bored," she said.

"How much would that be?" I asked quite interested.

"Two hundred and forty five dollars with seventy three cents since I last checked."

My jaw fell down.

"Impressed?" she said with a small smile.

"Yes, very much actually," I finished.

10

School. Just the very word hurt as much as if your molars were getting pulled out. But it would eventually come, I though as I groggily pulled on a pair of pants. After quite a slow bus ride we got there. It was like snapping back to attention. All that was missing was a humongous billboard saying *Welcome to Reality!*

The day was slow and negligent until third period, where I grasped the spiral on my notebook with sweaty hands. I stepped forward to the nasty desk where Mrs. Nacker sat. She did not look up from the tests she was correcting until she said, "How may I help you, Mr. Russell?"

"Hi, Mrs. Nacker. I was kind of wondering if you could review this. I′d like to have your opinion about it." I winced in my head.

"I′d be glad to!" she said.

Surprised by her response, I gave her my notebook speaking a soft, "Thank you," and she continued with the tests. That didn't make it very promising. "I mean it's short so far, you know-" I continued.

"Yes, Mr. Russell. But I'm sure you don't want to be late for lunch now do you?" she looked upwards at me over her giant spectacles.

"Uh, no. Well, I guess that's it then," I said.

I couldn't say anything else, so I turned on my heel and walked "calmly" out of the classroom. *That's it?* I thought. I nervously wondered what my teacher would think. *What if my mother was just being nice and saying good job, when it was really a botch?* My stomach leaped and lurched all the way to the cafeteria.

"Chase, your face is the color of paper! What's wrong, man?" said Gordon.

"Do you think it has something to do with what we've noticed?" Jack said in a mysterious voice.

"Noticed what?" I asked.

"Oh I don't know! Maybe it has something to do with Bailey," Sam said.

"And the staring," continued Gordon fluttering his eyelashes.

"And L-O-V-E," Jack spelled out.

"That is not-" I tried to excuse myself. Their looks made me blurt out, "Partially true?"

They all laughed and disapproved this answer.

"I like her as a friend but not love her!" the words were dry on me.

"All right then, prove it," Jack said.

"How would I do that?"

"By staying put right where you are even though she´s talking to Jeremy Hirsch and all her friends are giggly."

"How much do you want to bet?" I said roughly, stretching out my hand.

"Ten dollars," said Gordon.

"Five dollars."

"Seven dollars."

"Three dollars."

"Two fifty."

"Two fifty."

"Done!" we all said in unison. I shook hands with all three of them.

"Turn around," said Sam.

I easily flipped over to the direction required. I lost my color again. Bailey indeed was talking to Hirsch. *Oh god! Please don´t!* I exclaimed in my head. The ugly truth was that Hirsch was not at all bad looking, after all, all the girls in eighth grade fell for him. He had that bad boy charm, the kind even teachers fall for. And to add trash to the heap, he was quite smart and persuasive.

Bailey was in the shy-girl position. She was constantly shifting weight, working to and fro. Her arms were stiff and straight holding a notebook. MaryAnn, Isabella, and Natalie were unsuccessfully trying to hide behind a table that offered no true protection.

I returned to my initial position facing my friends. They all had playful smirks on their faces.

"Face it," said Gordon.

"Just give me the two bucks and keep your fifty cents," I said in a tight voice.

"You are saying that because you know we're right. Not like you can do much with two quarters anyway!" Jack said.

"Fine," I said.

The girls were coming our way now, whispering and gossiping about what had happened. We heard Is say, "He's cute!" We all fixed our expressions and acted like we didn't know anything.

"Ohmygod!" Is said all together.

They all crashed onto the table.

"Did you see that?" asked MaryAnn.

"See what?" Sam played along, messing with his pudding.

"Jeremy Hirsch was totally hitting on Bailey!" explained Natalie.

"Hmmm, no kidding!" I said peeling an orange a little too savagely, "Well, nothing we haven´t seen from Hirsch, now have we?"

All the girls, especially Bailey, looked confused, and Sam shot me a warning look, I´d gone too far.

On the bus, the first thing I said was, "Why did you even speak to him?"

"I don´t know. He was nice you know?" she answered.

"No, Bails. I don´t know!" I continued, "Listen, Hirsch is-"

"Not as bad as you think!" she cut me off. "He wanted to apologize about last time. He also offered buying me lunch, but I already had mine, so what was I supposed to do?" she said more to herself than to me.

"I can buy you lunch too, you know? Any other guy could! Why him?" I exclaimed.

"What the hell has gotten into you, Chase?"

I continued, "I could bet big money that he would poison your apple or something, and you´d drop dead like Snow White!"

"How do you know?" she questioned.

"Because I know Hirsch-"

"You know, you should really quit saying you know him if you haven´t even spoken to him," she defended.

"Why are you on his side?" I asked incredulously.

"I´m not taking any sides, Chase," she piped down.

"Says who?"

"Says me!" she snapped.

The second grader beside us had wide eyes and looked struck by our vigorous conversation.

I looked out the window, "Bails, listen-"

"No, you listen!" she said somewhat angry and frustrated, "He was nice to me and I´m not judging any books by their covers and if you can´t deal with it, drop my case Chase Russell!" At these last words she stood up and stomped off the bus. She looked seriously pissed off when she entered her house.

I was boiling up, steaming vapor coming out of my ears.

As I entered my house, I violently slammed my bag on the kitchen floor, and kept walking.

My mom looked up from the stove and said, "Hi, honey!"

I didn´t answer and instead flamed on into the small living room past the kitchen and lay down furiously on the couch.

Moms are moms, and they know their children as well as the palm of their hand, well, at least mine did. You could also read me easily, and I guessed that by now she knew exactly everything that had happened. She reacted instantly and walked over to me.

"Oh, honey what´s wrong?" she asked in an annoying sweetness.

“Nothing,” I answered dryly.

“Honey, I know this is really motherly but here it goes. I′ve noticed that you like Bailey, but, not just friend-like,” she began.

“Is anyone not going to tell me that today?” I gasped, moving the hand that was rubbing my forehead into the air.

The best shield I could find was a cushion which I placed on top of my face.

“Well, is there any way I can help you?” she asked.

“Unfortunately, no,” I finished in a sarcastic tone.

I heard my mother′s footsteps leave, returning to the kitchen. After a couple of minutes, I came out of hiding.

The next couple of days were filled with avoiding discussion. On the bus, Bailey sat way at the back and left me dangling alone in a far seat. At lunch time the girls started walking towards our table, and then got one of their own, ditching us. My friends were obviously mad at me too for the fight, but they still ate with me in total silence. On the other side of the road, my parents were having trouble again. Believe me, my mom′s lack of decision, my father′s stubbornness, impatience, and exhaustion don′t mix.

As I was doing my homework, I stood up, walked to the kitchen where my mother was putting dinner into containers so we could reheat it later, I said, “Mom, you are an experienced adult in life and I was wondering if maybe you could help me out with the problem,” She knew what I was talking about.

My mother beamed at my request for help. "Well, apologize," she answered shortly.

My temper took over me and I said, "Apologize? Ha! Why would I ever do that? She´s the one that´s making no sense and apologizing should be her job!"

"Well, darling, this is where that experience you were talking about comes in and even if you aren´t even a fraction guilty in any part of this argument, you should say sorry. Then the other person feels like you are right and apology accepted. *Wala!"* she affirmed.

"Should I call or walk over there?" I asked resentfully.

"Oh, calling is lame if you have her next door!" she said, a smile forming on her lips. "Run along now," she ended.

I opened the main door and stepped outside. The sky shinned beautifully with the frosty twilight that wrapped around our neighborhood. I reached the yellow house faster than what I had planned, but know, there was no turning back. I reached out and rang the doorbell.

Malcolm opened the door, "Hi, Mr. Gray." Before I could keep talking, Bailey appeared behind her father. Immediately, she tried to hide. Malcolm took a step to his left, and walked back into the house, and left Bailey standing there alone.

"Hey," I said. She did not answer. I cleared my throat, "So um, I came by to apologize about, you know, what happened," I continued, "If you like Jeremy, I´m okay with it. I mean, it is your decision on that. I got a little mad, but

I´ve got terrible temper, you know that right? You know what? I´ll buy you a bag of Skittles, how does that sound?" I said.

She unfolded her crossed arms, grinning slightly, "Apology accepted."

I didn´t answer with words, but I think my expression revealed all.

"Oh and you can save up that Skittle money," she said and giggled. She moved her hand onto her neck and held something.

"What´s that you´re holding?" I asked.

"Oh," she said pulling out a little silver circle with a chain holding it around. She held it between two fingers. "My dad gave it to me when I was like six or seven."

I noticed that it had some sort of inscription on it, but I couldn´t make it out. "What does it say?"

"Nothing really, unless you spin it," she said excitedly.

"Spin it?" I raised an eyebrow.

"Yeah, look," she said.

I moved closer. I saw a series of sticks and semicircles carved in, revealing nothing. Then with her finger, Bailey softly pushed the metal piece from the rim holding the sides. It started spinning madly, the little figures forming the word HOPE. I was hypnotized by the movement, until it finally came to a stop. "That is so cool!" I exclaimed.

"Yeah, well, I´ve got homework and stuff so-"

"Oh yeah! Me too, bye," I said.

"Bye," she responded.

I turned around and started walking towards the bending corner. After a couple of steps I looked back and Bailey was still in the doorway, arms crossed again. She waved and I waved back. I kept walking as I ran a hand through my hair. I eventually reached the corner and when I looked back- she was still there! Bailey didn´t notice that I saw her; and she smiled tilted her head, and finally entered her home. I was truly pleased by this. *Maybe she does like me after all,* I thought.

When she had tilted her head sideways, she had a dreamy look in her sapphire eyes as she looked at the twilight I had noticed previously. It was almost gone now. She was clearly thinking about something. Something that she desired or was pleased by but, what do I know?

I opened the door, when my mom was about to leave for work again.

"So how did it go?" she asked.

"It was good, actually," I said.

"And?" she continued eagerly.

"Apology accepted!" I said.

"I´m glad," she said.

Now, seeing Bailey reminded me of something I had been bothering me over and over in some of my sleepless nights.

"Why so gloomy? I thought you just got your friend back," my mother said.

"Mom, I´m worried about something," I began.

"Now what is it, honey?" she asked troubled.

"Well, I´ve already imagined people buying my book when it hits the shelves. I mean, I´ve already seen pictures of myself in some talk show answering questions some important and well known host asks. Oh god! I´ve even imagined it being turned into a movie! It´s- nuts," I finished. "And as much as I dream on and want to see people with my book in their hands, it´s practically impossible for me to get published."

"Oh darling, you can send it to a literature magazine or maybe get it printed and you can sell it at school," my mom suggested, "It´s a great start because honestly, what you´re saying is very true."

"Oh but mom, try to understand! I know that´s a great accomplishment but still I want the solid product. I want for something to be really real for maybe the first time in my life," I pointed out, "And then again, we hit the same wall. I´m thirteen years old! And there are many other authors out there that are so much better than me. They work so hard and some of them don´t get published! Where am I in this picture? How will I get out there?" I stated, signaling with my hand the outside world.

My eyes burned with warm tears, but I wasn´t going to cry like a baby! My mom came closer and embraced me in a tight hug. *NO!* I was seriously furious and frustrated by this. I felt ill and angry; *who does she think I am?* My state made me say this in a rough voice, “It′s impossible.”

My mom leaned in and whispered, “Nothing is impossible.”

11

"Here we are, dig in!" said Gordon while he opened a plastic Tupperware filled with mouth watering cookies. All of our hands shot forward, reaching out for the glorious goodness. I stuffed a cookie in my mouth.

"Wow! These are the chewiest, softest, chocolatiest, and greatest cookies ever!" Natalie said.

"I will send the compliments to the chef!" Gordon said, cookie in hand.

"I really want one! You know what? I′ll just take one of these, that should do it," Bailey smiled taking out a container.

"What′s that?" I asked.

"They are my new prescription pills. The doctor said it might even take the intolerance away!" she explained.

"So you might be able to drink milk again?" MaryAnn exclaimed.

"Yes I will!" Bailey said as she opened its cap.

"Is this the first time you take these?" MaryAnn questioned.

"Well yeah, Mare, I barely got them yesterday!" she answered in an almost incredulous tone.

Why is she so concerned? It's just pills, I thought.

Acting completely natural, Bailey reached into the small container, took a pill, and popped it into her mouth. She took a swig from her water bottle and gradually swallowed it.

We all kept eating and continued with our buoyant conversations. Suddenly, Bailey began to cough. Something made me think, *something smells fishy.* She kept coughing continuously, leading us all towards a slow silence.

"Whoa, don't choke on those chips now!" Jack joked.

"I don't think it's the chips, Jack," I said looking at her.

Bailey was gaining a color she had never even fantasized. She was sweating and panting between her dry coughs. I immediately grabbed the brown container and began skimming quickly through the ingredients this medication had. There were so many strange words like Croscarmellose Sodium and such.

"Are you allergic to any type of- any type of medicine or something?" I practically screamed at her.

She wheezed as she inhaled, shaking her head. She didn't try words, because words wouldn't come out of her throat. The rest of the table was already on their feet and heads from neighboring tables were turning.

"Come on, Bailey! You have to breathe!" Isabella said.

I didn´t care if we were at school or not, and my rising panic made me say the first thing that came to my mind, "Somebody call the hospital!"

Now everybody wanted to know what was happening. Principal Callaway walked through the door. When he saw that it was us that were causing all this commotion, he jogged over to us.

"What´s happening kids?" he asked confused.

"She´s choking, for god´s sake!" Natalie exploded in an urgent voice.

"I´ll call the nurse!" he exclaimed.

"The nurse? Don´t you mean the hospital?" Gordon said pointing at Bailey.

When he saw the horrid state she was in Mr. Callaway said, "Yes, very true!"

Now Bailey´s eyes were closing.

"Oh god, no! Come on, Bailey, wake up!" Isabella said slapping her face gently.

"She fainted!" Jack exclaimed.

We could hear the ambulance arriving.

"Let´s carry her to the entrance!" Sam suggested.

"On go, okay? One, two, three, go!" I said.

Isabella was in the front, moving spectators that were trying to get a better look at Bailey. "Move people!" she said. MaryAnn and Natalie were at her legs, Jack and Gordon held up her sides, and Sam and I were grasping her shoulders and head. She was heavier than usual because of her unconsciousness.

We finally reached the entrance and found the ambulance. Two nurses in baby blue uniforms awaited us as well. They opened the back doors and slid the crate out. Together, we all lay Bailey carefully on the thin mattress.

We began to get into the ambulance when Principal Callaway and some other teachers pulled us out.

"But she's our friend!" Sam said.

"Well, I'm sorry students but we can't let you go with her!" Mr. Callaway said.

I saw them close the doors, and then returned my glance to the Principal. "Why not?"

"Because, young man," he continued. The engine of the ambulance revved on, and the vehicle started driving away with it's terribly frustrating siren. "It would violate the hospital's rules, and besides, it's gone," he said dryly.

IT'S gone? Is he worried about the minivan or her? I exclaimed in my head. The bell rang, and the eighth grade teacher, Mrs. Wright, who was a black woman with thick, dark curls and deep green eyes said, "Come on kids, it's time for class."

We all turned and started to walk back. None of us spoke; we just exchanged looks of worry. I walked through the halls drenched in thought with a haunted expression.

"Chase! Are you okay?" I looked up. It was Mrs. Zelther.

With furious eyes I bit my lip, shook my head, and walked away.

In science class there was silent chatter about what had happened. Everything was in slow motion for me: the noise, the faces, the actions. I was the only one going at a true speed. I couldn′t think, because those thoughts hit me like soft bullets, constantly and painfully. My head was actually aching.

"Hey, Chase!" I heard a girl say. I looked up, and found Nikki Brightman. "Can you tell us how it really happened?" she questioned in an eager voice.

"I don′t know," I said more to myself than to Nikki.

"What about it?" Nikki kept shooting questions.

"Settle down, class," Mrs. Stein said, and the class began.

The fact that Bailey′s seat was vacant made me remember, so my stomach lurched. While I was wondering off into my own dimension, I heard, "Chase? The answer, please?"

"I′m sorry, which one, Mrs. Stein?"

"Relax, Chase. She′s going to be fine," Sam said.

We were now in our project groups, and we were stuck flipping pages in text books with Sarah Crouch, who did nothing but whine about how much she wanted to get her braces off.

"Yeah, I know," I said.

"I′m worried too you know," he admitted.

"Well, I guess we′ll just have to wait," I concluded.

Suddenly, we heard a loud snore that made us turn our heads. Sarah′s face was pressed to her notebook as she slept soundly. We both burst into laughter.

Sam poked her arm with a pen, "Sarah?" he said in between chuckles.

This time she snored even louder, which started us off again.

"Chase, I think-" laugh, "I think she′s dead!" Samuel said.

"Oh you know, science can really kill you," I said.

We kept on laughing for the rest of the class.

On the bus, there was no Bailey. I was nervous again, even after that great science period.

When I opened the door, my mom was sitting at the table, calmly reading a magazine. I wanted to tell her the news, but I choked.

"Honey, you look like you′re peeing your pants. Or *are* you actually peeing your pants?"

I chuckled, “I wish it were something that simple.” I pulled out the chair beside her, “Bailey had an accident today. She′s- she′s at the hospital,” I didn′t want to say anything else.

“How did it happen?” she gasped, “I had coffee with Janette this morning! Do you think she knows already?” my mom said.

“I hope so! If not, she must be going ballistic!” I thought.

“Well, we′ll pray for her tonight, won′t we?” my mother suggested.

“Yeah,” I nodded.

So I did. I usually went to sleep without praying, but this time I did as recommended. I got into bed, and made the sign of the cross. “Dear lord,” I began, “Take care of her. Please, permit her to be safe and healthy. I think I′m making a bigger deal of this than what it really is. But still, grant her peace in the hospital and illuminate the doctors that will treat her.” I took advantage of the fact that I had already begun praying, and continued, “Take care of my family and friends. Please, let them be happy and healthy. I pray for the countries that are struggling, whatever the struggle is, and help them so they will be able to move forward. Deliver us from poverty and- and,” my eyes began to close as I dozed off and them, WHAM!

Everything went black. I was sailing through darkness again, and then, it was déjà vu. I was running again. I groaned, tossed, and turned, over and over.

"Help!" I finally identified the voice that had appeared in this dream that I had experienced so often lately: Bailey. It was her in the house in flames. For the first time, the dream progressed more than just standing in front of the house. I ran towards it, the burning feeling of fire so near. With my foot, I kicked down the unstable door, and it fell to the ground.

"Bailey?" I screamed. I couldn't see anything because of the smoke as I heard someone cough, so I followed the sound. It seemed like it was coming from the ground. When I looked down, there laid Bailey, barely supporting herself with her hands. Her face was scratched and dusted with ashes. I wrapped my arm around her side and tried to pull her up. A piece of ceiling smashed down onto the floor, new flames being created. "Come on!" I yelled.

I started running as Bailey tried to keep up with me. We were both coughing now but I kept going. I took a step and tripped over something that violently flung us into the air. We flew through the door and crashed down on the street. We rolled until we reached a stop. She landed face up, and I the opposite. I ran my tongue over my lip. It tasted like blood. As I did this, Bailey coughed once more and her head dropped to the side, eyes closed. I heard the fire truck's siren as my head too, fell to the ground.

My legs were wrapped around my sheets. *God, these dreams are killing me! Ok, Chase, just relax and sleep,* I told myself. When I woke up in the morning I was thankful that it was Friday, the last day of the week. At school it was the same thing as yesterday, drifting away and preoccupation. What I needed was to write. I hadn't written in so long and I thought it was about time to restart. When I got home, I took out my notebook and these are little pieces of what I wrote:

Peter was perspiring in the hot burning sun. It was tiring to walk in the heavy sand, his sandals sinking deeply in the soft and golden ground.

"This- is- killing me!" Corggle said roughly

"Come on, Corggle! I´m a fairy and I have a lot less body mass than you, so let´s go!" Tiff said

The sun made the top of the sand dunes look glazed, like doughnuts. Peter began to see a green blur in the distance. He shaded his eyes from the powerful rays of the sun. When he squinted his eyes, the undefined figure became clear.

"Palm trees!" he exclaimed.

Tiffany and Corggle turned towards the direction Peter was pointing at.

"No, no. That can´t be it because I´ve read about this! It´s just an illusion caused by your desperate need of food and water, so you think there´s fertile land, shade, and the whole enchilada; but it´s not really true," Corggle explained.

"Well, we can at least try, right?" Peter suggested.

"All right, let´s go!" said Tiffany, and they began their journey to the mysterious green.

They walked and walked until they finally reached their goal. They overlooked the palm trees and shrubs and saw a glistening pool of crystal clear water.

“There’s water!” Tiffany pointed out.

“For the love of all that´s holy! When will you understand that it is just an illusion?” Corggle warned.

Peter reached out towards the palm tree in front of him. He ambiguously placed his hand on the rough trunk, not knowing what to expect.

“Hey, Corggle?”

“Yeah?” he answered.

“Can you feel an illusion?” Peter asked

“Technically, no. Illusions are things you imagine, they are not solid,” said Corggle.

“Then this is no imagination – it´s real!” Peter told them.

“It´s an oasis!” Tiff exclaimed.

Peter excitedly jumped over a little bush and moved forward to the water. Both his friends followed.

“Whoa, hold it! The plants might be real, but the water cannot be real. This time I´m 80% sure,” he calculated.

“We can try that too, just like the palm trees,” Peter said.

Then suddenly, some words began to form in the sand. It seemed like an invisible finger was tracing them. Peter and his friends began to read the message. It sounded like scribbling on paper. When the formation was finished, the sound stopped, and Peter read aloud, "To pull you in, three little drinks it´s all it takes, don't be foolish of your fates!" he finished. "What´s that supposed to mean?" he asked.

"I don't know," Tiffany said truthfully.

"Let´s try the water anyway!" Peter suggested.

He dipped his hands into the water and retrieved it. He neared it to his mouth and took a sip. The cool liquid running through his throat was explosively refreshing.

"It´s real too and it´s wonderful!" Peter announced.

Absentmindedly, both Tiffany and Corggle ran to the water´s edge and began to fiercely dig into their salvation. Corggle took one, two, three drinks and suddenly the oasis sucked him in. Tiffany followed and she too, drinking a third time disappeared as Peter washed his face. Lastly, Peter cupped his hands inside the water and drank his third and last gulp. There was a suctioning feeling all of a sudden. An inevitable pulling that was too hard to resist was what finally tugged him beneath the surface.

A splash of blue deep waters that were terrifically radiant formed what looked like a huge waterslide. This turned out to be a geyser. At first, Peter was afraid and bewildered, but was now having immense fun.

"Woo hoo!" he said, little bubbles flowing out of his mouth.

He looked down and there were Corggle and Tiffany, exclaiming in delight. Next, Corggle disappeared again and then Tiff. When Peter reached the disappearance point he felt the geyser push him upwards to what looked like a new surface. He was brutally spit into the air, and landed quite roughly on moist soil. He tasted the warm air and opened his eyes as a drop of water ran down his nose. The first thing he saw was every single type of plants you can imagine. A ray of sun shot through a tall and majestic tree, hitting a closed white flower. This one opened, showing its inner beauty.

"Where are we?" asked Tiffany, drying her wet, red hair.

"We´re in the jungle."

...They were swinging in the tree vines like Tarzan, Tiff flying freely beside them. Peter jumped to Corggle´s vine, surprising him. They swung back and forth several times. Suddenly they began to only move forward at full speed. They screamed together as their dear fairy friend tried to catch up to them.

"Boys, slow down! Be careful!" Tiffany shouted.

"We can´t! It´s like a giant zip line and it won´t stop!" Peter told her.

They were constantly being slammed by branches. Corggle caught a pomegranate in his mouth and the juice squirted out. They all began to laugh, but the humor didn't last long, when they saw a fat tree in front of them. They began to wrap around the trunk.

"Guys!" Tiff squealed.

When the vine was about to finish up, they were whipped out to the plants. Peter and Corggle slammed into a cold, hard wall. They slid down and finally reached some type of ground of the same substance.

"Peter, Corggle, are you okay?" Tiff urged.

"Uh, no. Not really. That´s the second time we fall on something hard, but we´re alive," Corggle responded rubbing his head.

A bone chilling breeze blew.

"Holy pine needles! It´s really co- cold!" Tiffany´s teeth chattered.

They were in the white, utmost glistening beauty ever. Majestic peaks of ferocious temperature and height rose over their heads. A nakedness and pure simplicity made this glacial paradise breathtaking...

... The fish that the polar bear, Bill, had provided them was no good now, for they had already eaten it and were desperate for food. They were headed towards the huge walruses before them, to see if they had anything edible. They finally reached them. They were so big, fat, wrinkled, and flabby. They´re humongous tusks were quite threatening.

"Um, hello," Peter attempted to salute.

A large, elderly male, with a bow tie and an eye glass, turned his head.

"We were wondering if you have anything for us to eat," Peter went on.

"Good evening. My name is Sir Nicholas, and we don't plan on giving you anything! We only have one pineapple and were an awful lot more walruses than you think," he complained with a thick British accent.

"Pineapple, Sir? How can you have a pineapple here? Did you go to the jungle?" Tiffany inquired.

"Oh my dear, of course not! They grow under the ice," he informed, which caused all the walruses to look down.

"Well, if they grow underwater, can´t you just give us the one you have and dive in for another one?" Corggle asked rudely, his stomach gurgling.

"Shhh, Corggle! Where did your manners go?" Tiffany scolded.

"What a disgrace that you should say that! I have now grown tired of you so get out of here!" the angry walrus said.

All the walruses began to walk forward.

"Excuse my friend! It´s just that he´s truly hungry but he really didn't mean it," Peter said, taking a few steps back.

The group of walruses kept advancing. "All right, flap!" Sir Nicholas ordered. The entire group of beast began to lift their flippers and slap down on the ice. Peter, Corggle and Tiffany were being pushed close to the icy edge. When they were about to fall into the freezing waters, there was a scary sound of a crack that finally created silence. No one talked, slapped or screamed. They began to look around searching for the birth place of the sound, that made the little hairs behind Peter´s neck stand up. It was useless, since the massive walruses retook their thunderous attempt to scare the visitors off.

Then, it happened once again, CRACK! The crack came from below Peter and his friends' feet. The solid looking ice was now braking apart from the big mass of land. The circle shaped piece of ice they were standing on started gliding on the freezing waters.

Although he was still in shock, Peter managed to say, "Farewell my friends!" to the awed animals.

Sir Nicholas robotically waved at them, as they were off into the deep blue...

...There was barely any ice left when they began to notice that the water under them was lighter and clearer. Suddenly a much unfocused image of a shoreline was barely visible.

"Is that what I think it is?" Corggle said in a tired voice.

Peter looked up, "It´s California!" he exclaimed.

They began to cheer, but they noticed the fate that was yet to come. It was soon time for farewell. They all grew quiet.

"Guys-"Peter began.

"Shhh, Peter. You don't have to say anything, really," Tiffany cut him off.

"But I want to," Peter continued, "you are one of the greatest things that has ever happened to me, and I can always visit, right?" he suggested.

"Yeah, I guess you´re right," Corggle said, trying to suppress tears.

"But you have to have your parent´s permission, of course!" Tiff added.

"Yes. I think that would be necessary," Peter stated with a chuckle.

He reached out for Corggle and gave him a big hug. His good friend sniffled. They reached the shore when Peter finished hugging Tiff. Now, the boy with the blue eyes and black hair jumped of the ice and said, "I'll see you guys later, good bye."

He walked to the beach. A warm breeze blew, and Peter heard the soft whisper of Tiffany´s voice, "Good bye, Peter- for now."

I was done. My pencil had stopped, as I sat there in awe. Suddenly, I snapped to attention. I jumped up with my notebook in my hands as I screamed, "I´m finished!" I ran out of the room. "Mom, I´m finished, I´m done!" I exclaimed when I got to the kitchen.

"What?" she said and took it for a second. She flipped some pages. A grin grew on her face, but she did not say anything. She pulled me into a violent hug, "I´m so proud of you!" she said.

Ben ran into the kitchen, "What´s with the screaming? What´s going on?" He was in a towel, and very wet.

"I am done, Ben, I´m done!"

He grinned, "Congrats Bro!" He patted my back.

My dad came up behind me, pulled me up on his firm shoulders and said, "I heard all the fuss! Chase, I´m so proud of you!"

Michael joined in, and we all celebrated.

"Well this is definitely an occasion for cake, right?" my mother said.

"But of course!" my father said.

It was at that moment, probably one of the few though, that I could actually say my family was in harmony. Dad wasn't complaining about money, or mom of the weather, I wasn't fighting with Ben, and Mike wasn't thinking about something else. We were truly a family.

We finished enormous chunks of my prize, coated in my mom´s lemon zest frosting, since it was her exquisite recipe for Carrot Cake. Yum!

12

I was nervously bopping my legs up and down, my notebook in my hands. Gosh, how uncomfortable these plastic chairs were! Silence ruled over all of us, except crying babies being consoled by their mothers. The walls were painted in bright colors, attempting to make us feel better. But who could ever feel good in a hospital?

I was alone since my mother had gone to visit a friend who had broken some ribs. Suddenly, a girl from the row behind me stood up and walked up to my spot, and sat next to me.

“I′m guessing you′re Chase?” She was beautiful, around sixteen years old, and looked extremely familiar, but I couldn′t put my finger on it.

“How′d you know?” I asked astonished.

“Partly because you fit my sister′s descriptions and the rest was just a lucky guess!” she said, “Emma Gray.”

“Bailey′s sister then?” I asked.

"Yup. What´s that?" she pointed at my notebook with a nail polished finger.

"That´s my book, I mean, our book," I said, referring to Bailey and me.

"So that´s why she drew all that stuff!" Emma realized, "So, what´s up?"

"Well, I´m here to visit your sister. I´m guessing you are too," I began.

"Yeah but, who´d you come with ´cause they give you a hard time about being up here alone," she said.

"My mom´s visiting a friend of hers."

"What happened to her?" Emma asked.

"Broke some ribs," I explained.

"Guess it´s a lot tougher than some allergy, right?" she said with a bitter grin.

"Were you worried about her, you know, Bailey?" I questioned.

"Well, yeah," she said, "she is my sister, and the only one I have for that matter. We were close to losing her once. Don´t want it to happen again."

"Really? How? Tell me ´bout it," I said.

"When she was about, six or seven everything changed. It all began with the fevers, the nose bleeds, and the paling skin. They discovered she had mild case of acute lymphocytic leukemia. I can perfectly remember one day, when she walked into my room and said, `What´s going to happen to me, Emma?′ She looked so weak and dull. All I was able to do was to grasp her into a tight hug, and held back my tears. All the therapies and everything-" she choked. "Luckily, her case was cured. Now even a little scratch scares us all."

Every little piece fell into the puzzle. The "HOPE" necklace Bailey′s father had given her, the jelly jars full with money, her pale skin. "That explains a lot," was all I said.

"Yeah, it′s kind of weird I told you all of this just like that. I barely know you," she said.

I chuckled, "I guess you just know you can trust me," I said.

A chubby nurse came into the scene. "You can see your little friend now, darling," she said.

I stood up, "It was great meeting you, Emma," I said.

"You too. And, Chase," I turned around, "your pretty good, after all," she told me with a grin, and I walked down the hall.

The nurse opened the door, and I stepped inside as she closed it behind me. Bailey lay in her bed surrounded by balloons and gifts from previous visitors. She turned her head towards me and took my breath away with her impeccable smile.

"Hey there, partner," I said recovering.

"Hey," she answered.

There were no chairs in the room, so I walked over to the edge of Bailey's bed, awkwardly standing there. I cleared my throat and said, "So, how've you been?"

"Better, I guess. I get out tomorrow, doc told me," she answered.

"Well, that's good," I said shortly. My head was too busy documenting everything that Emma had told me. Bailey was as ghostly white as she was described by her sister.

"What are you thinking about?" she read my expression.

"Um, homework," I lied.

She cocked an eyebrow upwards, "Chase Russell, you are a terrible liar."

I laughed nervously, "I guess so."

"So what were you thinking about?" she still inquired. When she saw I did not plan on replying, she said, "Guess I don't look too good, do I?"

"Are you kidding? If you're getting out tomorrow, then you're fit as a fiddle. All you need is some sunlight," I teased. She laughed a little. My legs began to ache.

"Are your legs getting tired?" she guessed correctly again.

"Nah, just a bit. Don't worry 'bout it," I tried to say in a light and effortless voice.

"You can sit on the edge of the bed if you like," she gestured towards her feet.

I did as she suggested. The bed wasn´t as uncomfortable as people said they were.

"You know, it hasn´t been easy to be in here," she said.

"Why?" I questioned.

"Well, as you may have noticed I´m not the healthiest person in the world so I've been in a hospital before. This place reminds me of times in my life that weren´t so pleasant, let us say."

Oh boy, I thought.

"When I was little-"

"You were sick," I accidentally spilled out.

"How´d you know?" she protested in a low voice.

I exhaled, "Emma told me, a couple of minutes ago, outside."

"You met Emma?" she asked befuddled.

"Mhmmm. How hard was it?" I popped the question cautiously.

"Hard enough," she answered briefly, her eyes closed.

The mattress might have been comfortable, but my position was not. I had to twist my torso to be able to see Bailey. As I began to search for a new and more accommodating position, I made the springs on the bed screech.

"You´re still uncomfortable, aren´t you?" Bailey said with her eyes still closed.

I abruptly stopped my ruckus and said, “Yeah, I think so.”

We both laughed. “You can lie down if you want to,” she said, but we both knew very well that that would be an awfully awkward situation. But what was I supposed to do? “Do you think we´ll fit?” I asked.

“I think so,” she answered.

I shoved my body to the right, kicked up my legs, and lay my head on the pillow.

“Better?” she said.

“Yes,” I said closing my eyes just like she had.

I turned my head towards her. God, we were too close. “So,” I said returning to the ceiling.

“So,” she replied.

“I brought something for ya,” I took the notebook and gave it to her, “It´s done.”

Her jaw fell open. “What? It is done? Like we have our actual book?”

“Yup,” I answered.

“Oh my god! Chase, we did it!” she shrieked in excitement as I laughed.

We hugged each other, proud of our achievement.

“We´ve got to submit this to the publisher tomorrow!” Bailey said.

"But, Bails, tomorrow is your first day out of the hospital! Don´t you want to rest?" I reasoned.

"Rest? Please! That´s all I´ve been doing for the last seventy two hours!" she claimed.

"Well, if you say so," I said.

"And how´s your family?" she asked.

I had a flashback of my dad, two days ago. I walked past the living room, and saw him sitting on the couch, reading some bills with his glasses on. He cursed and swore at the paper as he slammed his pen onto it. "Nothing to write home about," I explained shortly.

"Not so good then, I´m guessing?" she questioned shyly.

"You could say that."

"Well, you don´t have to worry now. We´ve got this," she said tapping the surface of my notebook.

"Depends," I said dryly.

"Why the negativity? You´re too good not to get sold," she flattered me.

"Hey, aren´t you going to give yourself a little credit?" I asked.

"Come on, Chase, all I did was sketch up some drawings. No big deal," she shrugged.

"No, you did much more than that."

"And what would that be?"

"The characters just seem to come alive," I began, "and as cheesy as this sounds, they kind of make me alive."

We were so close, our noses almost brushed each other. My stomach was twirling. As Bailey came closer to me, the door opened with a loud click that snapped us apart and made me resettle into a sitting position.

"Honey, it´s time for you to go now," the nurse said.

I opened my closed, frustrated eyes and turned to her. "Yes, thank you. Just give me a minute," I said as kindly as possible.

She grinned and left.

I returned towards Bailey. "Uh, bye. I hope you feel better," but I wasn´t looking at her. My expression was puzzled as I left the room without a word.

"Holy cow, Chase!" Sam exclaimed.

"You almost kissed her?"Gordon said.

"You heard what I said, guys!"

"Chase, this is critical information! It is not just *something,*" Jack said.

I just kept chewing my cereal.

"But I mean, what was it like?" Gordon asked.

"First of all, it did not happen! But it was- weird. Everything else just dissolved away. It was just us. The feeling was kind of a mix of excitement and fear all at the same time. The truth is, I can´t really explain it," I said shaking my head.

"Dude, you´re a writer!" Sam said.

"Shut up!" I replied as we all laughed.

"I mean, Shakespeare did say, `Journeys end in lovers' meeting´!" Gordon said matter-of-factly.

There was a honk from a car outside.

"Mm! Tat´s go´ta ba ma mowm," Jack said between mouthfuls of cereal. He finished it up. "See you guys! And tell your mom thanks for me ´cause I really have to run!" he said.

"All right, see you!" I responded.

"And what else did she say?" Sam continued.

"Jeez, guys! It was nothing! Get over it!" I said.

"Excuse me but that was anything but nothing!" Gordon exclaimed.

"Okay, fine! I didn´t expect it, and it was pretty crazy because of that! Happy?" I stated.

"But good crazy, right?" Samuel grinned.

"Well- yeah."

We kept talking for a while, in which Sam confessed he liked MaryAnn and Gordon said he thought Isabella was, "Hoooooooooooot!" in his words, but he said he didn´t really like- like her. It was good to know I wasn´t the only one with troubles! Soon enough, they left, and I went to bed. My mind still tossed and turned with Bailey´s past, and our future.

***

"www.wrightmanbooks.com, enter," I said.

"What do you think they'll ask for?" Bailey asked excited.

From the moment she had entered my house, we didn´t and couldn´t even comment about what had happened the day before. We acted completely normal, all though we both knew very well that we were simply pretending.

The screen filled up with the homepage. We had already read the entire website together, in other occasions, so all we had to do was scroll down to the little blue link that said *Submissions.* Some months earlier we had agreed to read anything except the submission guidelines until we had the book ready. This of course, was simply to add more suspense to the whole deal.

"Okay, here we go. Welcome to Wrightman Books," I began reading, "Please review the box below with guidelines for your submission, depending on what type of book your novel is."

I moved down to find the fiction novel. It said in this chart that we needed to send our first three chapters, a summary of what happens later on in the book and the ending, and lastly, why we thought our book should be published. I looked at Bailey, "Shall we do it?"

"We shall!" she answered.

I had already passed onto the computer my first five chapters, which had been revised by Mrs. Nacker. We went to the document, checked it one last time, and started printing up to chapter three. We joyfully ordered the papers and stuck the copies of Bailey´s drawings where we wanted them to be. The website had said not to send the original illustrations in case anything happened to them.

We joined them with a paper clip, and opened a new document.

"We should introduce ourselves," Bailey suggested.

"Okay: Dear Sirs, Our names are Bailey Gray and Chase Russell," I spoke as I typed.

Together we composed a well recited and complete summary of what we had planned the end to be, and it all sounded quite professional. Then came the next part: Why was this book worth publishing? There was a moment of silence. The website required that we write the question and then the answer below it, so we did as we were told. I typed it down, and reread it. *Why is this book worth publishing?*

I turned to look at Bailey, who was staring at the screen. Then she turned her head to look at me. We were both thinking the same thing. The website said we should write one full paragraph, but our answer was; *It is fun, moving, and a story worth knowing.* That was it. Those words spoke everything they meant, and that was good enough.

I clicked on the icon with the printer sign on it. When it was done, Bailey attached that single page on top of the book, pushed it into the yellow envelope, and sealed it. We were so proud of ourselves, so happy. My mom drove us over to the post office, where we got in line, and sent it off to New York. We barely talked on the way back. We just made comments like, "I hope they like it," and, "How fast do you think it'll get there?" But our last words were, "So now we wait?"

"Now we wait."

13

It was dark, the street lamp glowing feebly. I walked silently; last thing I wanted to do was to wake up the whole neighborhood at this late hour. The blanket full of things was heavy over my shoulder as I reached the tree where Bailey was straightening out her blanket, the rest of her things beside her. "Will I *ever* arrive before you do?" I asked when I got there, dropping my luggage noisily.

"Shhh! Never!" she said.

We both giggled under our breath. I slipped out the blanket from under the supplies and laid it out next to Bailey's. Three weeks had passed since we sent our submission. Nothing really exciting or new had happened, just the usual. School, home, and waiting. Well, the Red Socks won a game, if that counts. On Friday, I had called Bailey with no hello, just a quick, "Meet me at midnight!" And I hung up.

So here we were, at midnight. We both sat down.

Bailey said, "Junk food."

"Check."

"Peanut butter?"

"Check."

"iPod?"

"Check!"

I plugged the iPod into the portable speakers, and pressed the play button. We rested our backs on the large tree trunk (our favorite), and stretched out our legs.

"So, I´ve noticed that Sam kind of likes MaryAnn, right?" Bailey began.

"How´d you know?" I asked.

"He´s just a little bit obvious," she said.

I just laughed a little and said, "Yeah." I could only hope that I wasn´t as obvious as Samuel was.

We were listening to ABBA, and the next song came up. I immediately recognized the melody, and began to sing the first words, "I was sick and tired of everything, When-"

"I called you last night from Glasgow!" Bailey joined.

"You know this song?" I questioned.

"Yeah, my parents sang this at home all the time," she said matter of factly.

"Really? Well then I´m guessing you know the chorus?" I said.

"Mhmmm!" she answered excitedly.

"Tonight's a super trouper lights are gonna find me shinning like the sun! Smiling, having fun! Feeling like a number one!" We sang together. We laughed as the song went on without us.

"Chase, who do you like?" Bailey asked, taking a bite on a gummy worm.

"Um, no one that would like me back," I answered shortly.

"What? That's a dumb answer! Who wouldn't like you? I mean, you're a good friend," she ended awkwardly.

"Well, how about you?" I said, desperately hoping that the subject would be changed.

"He wouldn't like me," she copied my words.

"How do you know?" I said, "What if the girl I like is standing right in front of me?" I spilled out.

"What if the guy I like is standing right in front of me?" She said.

There was silence. We stared at each other for a moment. My stomach was going crazy. I was trembling of adrenaline inside, and I had an entire zoo stampeding in my belly. It was like I was made of jelly. We closed up and, boom. It happened. The suspenseful moment in a movie, and the dream of any girl. It lasted a few seconds that seemed like a million years.

When we broke apart, Bailey said, "I had never done that before," Her eyes were closed and her eyebrows were pulled together. She relaxed her features and opened her eyes.

"Me either," I admitted.

"So that was the first kiss," she said a grin on her face.

"I guess so," I said.

We were both flaming red of embarrassment.

"You know, MaryAnn does like Sam, but you can´t tell anyone!" she said.

"I won´t, I won´t," I said. But deep inside, I knew I´d end up telling him. If I didn´t, nothing was going to happen!

All though this comment seemed a little uncomfortable for the situation, it was the icebreaker. We talked as we dipped our fingers into the peanut butter jar. The double dipping rule was not followed in this case. We sang to ABBA and told jokes and childhood stories.

I was laughing heavily as Bailey began another of her tales, "When I was younger, I was obsessed with Kim Possible! You know the cartoon they used to play on Disney Channel?"

"I actually remember that!" I chuckled.

"Well, Kim had this like, awesome rappel kit where she tied the ropes to her waist, and then clipped the other end to any surface. She could climb up a wall or climb down both. So, I thought that I could do this too. I tied all my jumping ropes and shoelaces together to make my rope. So I went to the balcony in my room and tied my rope to one of the poles and the other side around my waist. Luckily, when I was about to jump off the balcony so I could rappel down my house, my mother walked outside to put some lemonade glasses on the small white table. When she saw me she screamed, "Bailey! Get down from there, young lady, you're going to kill yourself!"

I began to laugh hysterically. "You actually tried that?"

"Yes!" she laughed as well.

We went on like that the entire night, until we fell asleep. I groggily woke up with my arm around Bailey's shoulder, and her head was resting on my own. It was dark, but the colors around me made me think that it would soon be dawn. I shook Bailey softly, "Bails! Hey, Bails wake up!" I whispered.

She lifted her head slowly with half closed eyes, and her hair was a mess. "Huh?" she said straightening up.

"You've got to wake up, it's almost dawn."

"Okay, uh-" yawn, "let's pick our stuff up and get going," Bailey said.

I closed the peanut butter jar and put the rest of the stuff on top of my blanket. I grabbed all four corners and joined them together to be able to carry it. We both pulled our "sacks" onto our shoulders and started walking back. When we reached our splitting point I said, "Well, you have something new to tell your girlfriends."

"What's that?" she said still sleepy.

"That you got yourself a boyfriend!" I told her. I turned around and started walking home happily.

"Are you asking me?" she said behind me.

"Goodbye, Bailey Gray!" I teased. I could feel her smiling behind me as I turned left. I reached my house, which I entered very quietly, and put the things back in their place. Upstairs I changed into my pajamas and went to bed, falling asleep a second time.

I woke up in a daze of unsteadiness; everything that had happened was a blur, like it wasn't real enough. I slowly slipped out of bed, rubbing my eyes. I went downstairs drowsily, and walked outside to the mailbox. I opened the little door and took out the filling. There was a bunch of letters, and I started shuffling through them. *No, no, no, no, n-.* I stopped. I couldn't believe my eyes. In small writing I read Chase Russell and Bailey Gray. I let out a loud scream.

My family ran outside, "What's wrong?" my mom squealed.

"It's- it's here!" I exclaimed.

"What is?" Michael asked.

"My submission letter!" I was about to violently rip it open, when I realized this was not only mine. I dialed Bailey's number and said, "Hello?"

I got lucky, Bailey had picked up. "Chase?"

"Bailey come to my house immediately, the letter is here!" She hung up before I had and was here seconds later.

We opened the envelope and began to read the following:

Mr. Russell and Ms. Bailey Gray,

We are truly pleased and impressed with the work that you have shown us. We believe that the story, the plot, and the sequence are original and complete. I quote, "It is fun, moving, and a story worth knowing." Congratulations! We are now about to make "The Ride" a published novel. We will soon contact you to discuss the process of publication. Well done! All the best!

Beth Collingsworth

Publishing Consultant

"Oh my god!" Bailey said.

"We are in!" I exclaimed joyfully.

My mother was so excited; she wanted to frame the letter. "We should show this to Mrs. Nacker on Monday! She´ll be so happy for us!" I said.

"Yeah! And we have to tell Gordon and Natalie and everyone!" Bailey said.

Success was in the air, and for once I felt like I had really done something for myself, and I wasn´t standing alone.

***

"*Strangers waiting up and down the boulevard their shadows searching in the night! Streetlights, people! Living just to find emotion. Hiding somewhere in the night!*" the radio sang the popular Journey song.

"I can´t believe that you guys did it!" Gordon said, "I´m just going to walk into a bookstore and I´ll see it on a shelf?"

"Yep!" I answered joyfully.

"That is insane!" MaryAnn exclaimed.

"It is so cool!"

I heard footsteps behind me, and everyone fell to silence.

"Mr. Russell, Ms. Gray," I heard. It was the deep, husky voice of Principal Callaway. "Please, come to the office with me. It´s just take a couple of minutes," he grinned.

We both stood up, exchanging looks of misunderstanding. All of our seated friends were also confused and silent. We started walking towards the office, which was simply not my favorite place in the world. I´ve always been afraid of getting in trouble, and this was the place where you were accused for it. We entered through the door and the secretary looked at us over her desk. It was terribly quite, and her glance focusing on us did not move, all though she kept typing something onto her computer.

"Good morning, Mildred!" Mr. Callaway said cheerfully.

She just raised a hand to signal that she had heard his words, and then turned to reach out for a tissue. She blew her nose loudly.

"Right this way, please," he showed us to his office.

I just nodded and Bailey followed. As we walked into the small room, our principal closed the door behind us, and walked over to his desk. He started putting some papers that lay on his desk away into a drawer, adding even more pressure to the moment. Bailey and I just stood there.

"Sit," he said pointing towards the chairs in front of him.

We followed his orders and waited for him to talk.

"First off, you are not in trouble," he explained.

My tense muscles relaxed and I let out a long breath.

"I have heard from a couple of birdies that you two wrote a novel that is having quite success-"

"Would it be okay if I asked who these people are?" I said as my curiosity caught up to me.

"None you should worry about. And it´s fine, you can ask anything you want here," he continued, "Well, I was thinking when I overheard your conversation this morning, that since this novel of yours is going to be published- which I think is an extraordinary accomplishment- I am truly proud-" he kept going.

Just get to the point! I thought in my head.

"- That you should make a presentation to the entire middle school of your book. We can make it like a little interview if you want. Teenagers like you might like to know about this!" he finished.

I broke out into a joyful chuckle, "Yes, I mean, that would be great!"

"All right. Let´s plan this, and you don´t have to worry about being late to class, I'll give both of you a pass so you will be excused," he said.

We went on for about twenty minutes, making questions and setting everything up.

"So we are scheduled for next week," he told us.

When we were done, he shook both of our hands and escorted us to class.

14

I took a deep breath, my eyes shut tight. *Relax, Chase, breathe,* I told myself. I opened them in a blur of nerves and people. *The entire Middle School-*

"Chase! C´mon let´s go!" Bailey said.

I reacted violently turning my head, my eyes finding her, and her extended hand.

"Why?" I said nerve wrecked.

"Principal Callaway called us up! Let´s go!" she said.

I took a couple of shaking steps. There was some clapping, but people were talking and were pretty much oblivious to our presence. No one was really paying attention, and probably didn´t care. The closer we got to the middle of the stage, the silence grew stronger, and everybody was completely quiet. The stage was set up like a talk show. Two chairs for us, a table in the middle with three glasses of water, and the third chair in front of us was occupied by Mr. Callaway. Personally, I thought our principal had overdone it this time.

We moved forward and sat on the chairs.

"All right! Well, today we are- as you all know- going to have an interview with two very special students; Chase Russell and Bailey Gray."

The crowd clapped weakly. At the back we could see our friends with excited expressions on their faces jumping and waving.

"So let´s get this show on the road! My first question for you is: What is it that you did?" he read from the paper.

"We wrote a book together," Bailey answered.

"And what got you started?"

I had forgotten I had a microphone in my hand. "Well, originally, it was only me. I enjoy writing very much and I decided I´d take advantage of that and bring it to a whole other level," I answered.

"Did it have anything to do with earning money?" Mr. Callaway added.

"It´s not the only reason but it´s part of it." That was another way to say that I needed the money for my family, but I also did it for pleasure.

"All right then! Next question: What is the title of the book?"

"The Ride," I responded.

"That's actually really catchy! The following question is more towards our illustrator," he nodded towards Bailey, "Do you think that your drawings help the story?"

I passed the microphone to Bailey. "Um, yeah. I believe that the drawings are kind of the helping hands of the words because it´s like what you´re imagining is on paper and it gives you a feel of what the characters look like and the settings," Bailey explained.

What an answer! I thought.

"And what is your story about?" Our principal asked.

Bailey passed the microphone onto me. "Well, the main idea is that one day this boy, Peter, is pulled by a strong current into the ocean and ends up in this magical island. Here, he meets two friends who will help him find his way home in a really crazy adventure."

"That sounds good! And how could you finish it so quickly?"

"I guess I have too much free time!" I answered.

The crowd laughed, so I felt a little more comforted. Throughout the presentation they became more and more interested, and it passed so quickly, we were suddenly in the last question.

"Okay, time to finish up. Are we going to see you around here when you are all rich and famous?" Mr. Callaway joked.

"I guess so!" I chuckled.

"All right! Give them a hand!"

Everyone clapped so loud there was an echo in the building. We walked down the stairs on the stage.

"So that wasn´t that bad!" Bailey exclaimed as she gave me a quick hug.

All of our friends were even more excited than they used to be.

"You guys were great!" Natalie said.

"You nailed it!" Jack added.

When we walked through the hallways, students of all grades were either congratulating us, or asking us more questions. I thought I heard someone say, "Are you guys doing book signing here? That would be so cool!" I just nodded without knowing where it had come from. I shuffled through a congratulating sea of people. Justin Tanenbaum, a very popular eighth grader was walking by. When he saw me, he raised his hand for a high five. I slapped back.

"Hey, good job, man!" he said.

"Thanks!" I responded, but he had already walked past me.

15

"School's almost over!" I said.

"I know! It's gone by so quickly!" Sam said.

Jack put his hand inside the bag of chips and stuffed a handful into his mouth indifferently. He didn't say anything.

"What are you guys doing this summer?" Gordon asked.

"Well, I'm going over to my cousin's. My mom wants me to do more outdoorsy stuff," Sam said.

"Where do they live again?" Jack questioned.

"Colorado," Sam answered shortly.

Samuel plus mountains- not the best combination.

"I'm going to go on a family trip for a couple of days, then I'm coming back," Gordon said.

"I´m going to go to a sports camp in Boston. It´s only two weeks, though," Jack said, "How 'bout you, Chase?"

"Staying here, I might help my dad with anything he needs, play some ball with Mike," I said.

It was easy to say this with my friends. They respected my situation, and I knew they weren´t here to judge me.

"You better remember us when you're all rich and famous!" Sam said.

"Of course I will!" I exclaimed.

"You better!" Gordon added.

"What was the name of your book again?" Jack asked.

"The Ride," I answered.

"Right! I knew that!" he excused himself.

The silence was awkward as we waited for someone to speak.

"Well, our conversation is very extensive!" Gordon said sarcastically.

We all laughed.

"We have been talking for a while. What else is there to talk about?" Jack said.

"What teachers do you want next year?" Sam said.

"Definitely Mrs. Wright for math! I´m done with Copmik!" I said.

"What about science?" Gordon asked.

"Rollins," we all said together.

Turns out that that teacher was not very strict, yet you learned enough in his class to pass the test. On the other hand, Mrs. Carver was so tough, people suspect she was in the navy.

"I don´t think I know any others," I said.

"There´s that Emerson lady for English," Jack said.

"True. I wonder if she´s vicious too," Gordon wondered.

"Deep inside, they all are," Sam commented.

"What time is it?" Gordon said.

"Whoa, nine thirty already? Looks like we have to leave *rapido*!" Jack said.

"Cool, we´ll see you tomorrow, man," Gordon told me.

They all stood up slowly, stretched out, and left through my front door.

The bell rang, followed by loud cheers and screams of joy. School was over, and we were done here. I thought about the year. There were so many memories that would last long after I left this building. The hallways were crammed with the buzz of farewells. My grin was bitter-sweet when I saw Sam in the middle of the crowd.

I moved through a couple of people and told him, "Let´s meet outside, try to tell everyone!" He just nodded and started moving towards his locker. I caught sight of Bailey, "Bails! Tell the girls to meet outside!"

"Okay!" she said over the people.

I reached my locker. I turned the knob on the lock until it clicked open. I grabbed the two remaining notebooks that filled this compartment, which now made it completely empty. I started closing the door. When it was ajar, I realized that not only was there no need to close it, but this was also the last time I used it.

When we were all finally outside, we started saying our goodbyes. The girls began to cry, as they always do. Us guys, we know that we'll see each other in what, like two or three months? We just gave a strong slap on the back and said, "Hey, we'll see each other soon!" I said goodbye to all of the girls except for Bailey, after all, she was on my bus.

We all walked to the bus area together giving our last quick goodbyes as we all parted our own ways. Bailey and I started heading towards our bus, but I suddenly stopped walking.

"What's wrong?" Bailey asked.

"Nothing," I answered.

"Then why'd you stop walking?" she said.

"I don't think I'm going back home on the bus," I continued, not knowing where all of this was coming from.

She raised an eyebrow and a grin, "What, is your temper raging?" she taunted.

"No, not yet," I replied.

"Just another one of those weird and inexplicable actions?"

"Most likely."

"So this is goodbye then," I said, but I really didn´t want to go.

"For now, at least. You want to know something?" she asked.

"Even if I said no you would still tell me, so why bother asking?" I grinned.

"Fine then! Well, you wouldn´t believe it but at the beginning of the year, I thought you hated me," she said.

I looked at her when she said this.

"I´m really glad we got along after all," she said. "And this is the part where I should probably repeat *again* for the millionth time how grateful I am to you for helping me through the year and how I really thank you for getting me across my cancer thing and missing California," she said in a funny tone, "Why did you do all of that for me again?" she said.

I chuckled. The buses started to honk behind us. Bailey started walking towards them, then stopped and ran back to me.

"Hey, see you when I see you?" she asked like we had many times before.

I hugged her, "Yeah," I kissed her cheek and let her go. She walked towards the buses again, waved goodbye, and then finally ran all the way.

I smiled to myself. I walked over to the road, and started walking down the bike path. I reflected on what I thought at the beginning; *this is a place where nothing changes, and not much happens.* I guess something did happen this time, didn´t it?

EPILOGUE

-6 months later-

Snap! The camera flashed and hurt my eyes. My hands were sweating as I grasped my own copy of, "The Ride." Bailey stood next to me, as well as Ronald Thorpe, Chief Editor of Wrightman Books and Beth Collingsworth, our Publishing Consultant. My mother looked at the screen, "Looks great!"

I remembered how a couple of months ago, when I had my book actually published, I was amazed by my achievement, but it was unbelievable where I was standing right now. We were actually going to appear on local news! The anchorman's name was Theodore Montgomery, and his phrase was, "Good evening, Winesburg. My name is Theodore Montgomery, but please- call me Teddy!" This man was a guy with fair sandy hair, and a thick mustache and eyebrows which seemed a bit out of place since they were darker than his hair.

They showed us to our seats behind the large table.

We were received by a jolly, "Hello, kids! I´m Teddy, maybe you´ve seen me on TV before," and he shook both of our hands.

"Rolling!" the camera man said.

Teddy straightened up and we followed.

"Five, four, three, two-" He signaled the start.

"Good evening, Winesburg! Welcome to Infonews here on Channel five. I´m Theodore Montgomery, but please-call me Teddy. Tonight, our first report is quite interesting. Here we have our guests, Chase Russell and Bailey Gray!"

The camera moved towards us. I just grinned and played around with my hands.

"So, these young teenagers just wrote a novel together that is now a successfully published book, so tell us about it!" he said enthusiastically.

"Well, our book´s name is ´The Ride, ´ and as you said it has been published by Wrightman Books. We would like to thank Mr. Ronald Thorpe and Beth Collingsworth for all of your help and support. It is now in bookstores or you can get it online. And well, I am the author and Bailey here is the illustrator," as I said this, I realized that not only had Bailey illustrated my book, but she had also illustrated my heart.

Lightning Source UK Ltd.
Milton Keynes UK
18 August 2010

158598UK00001B/5/P